Prayerful PREY

A Christian Abduction Thriller by
STEPHANIE HOLBROOK

To my lover and best friend, Donald.

Thank you for always being my safe harbor, my knight in greasy Carhartts, my place of rest in the midst of life's storms. The calm to my chaos. One thing at a time, Babe. Together.

A Christian Abduction Thriller

Prayerful PREY

One

"Mama, I wan' 'offee." Millie toddled up to Shiloh's side of the bed.

Why? Shiloh griped inside. *Why can't these kids sleep in on a Saturday? It's the only day we can!*

Resigned, Shiloh opened her eyes, blinking away the bliss of sleep. She focused on her youngest child whose nose barely cleared the mattress of her and Harbor's queen-sized bed. Waiting as patiently as she could, two-year-old Millie rubbed her eyes with the back of her plump little hand.

"*...body of missing woman, Jenna Jarvis, was found in an abandoned field...*"

An attractive auburn-haired news reporter in a baby pink blazer gave her report standing in front of a field. Behind her, logging trucks zoomed past and policemen unrolled crime scene tape. Shiloh found the remote and turned it off, not interested in hearing such dreadful news on a Saturday morning.

"Mamaaaa, I wan' 'offee!" Millie whined, her patience dissipating.

"Okay, baby," Shiloh whispered and slid out of the bed, careful not to disturb Harbor.

Millie led the way through the living room kicking through scattered stuffed animals, discarded kids clothing, and gummy snack wrappers. Entering the dining room, Shiloh glanced at the table, littered with half-empty water bottles contaminated with floating food particles and forgotten cups of sweet tea, the ice long melted. Scraps of supper resisted by picky eaters speckled the dark walnut-stained table. Shiloh's shoulders dropped even further; had her arms been longer, her knuckles would have dragged the ground in defeat.

When they reached the kitchen, Millie pulled close her wooden stepstool with chipped red paint. White lettering across the planks read, "This little stool is mine. I use it all the time. To reach the things I couldn't, and lots of things I shouldn't."

"I wan' do it, Mama!" Millie stomped back and forth before climbing atop her stool, fearful her mother would deny her the pleasure of pushing the start button.

"Chill out, Millie." As often as Shiloh had to tell her that, Millie ought've been as cold as the tundra of Antarctica. "I'm gonna let you." Shiloh fished a coffee pod from the drawer and then reached overhead for a coffee mug from the cabinet.

"No, no, I don' like dat un." Millie shook her head, her face a scowl.

"Millie," Shiloh groaned and turned her gaze upon her, "we're not doing this this morning. What cup do you want?"

"I waaannnn dat un." Millie's short finger pointed to the Valentine's Day cup. Shiloh pulled it down to fix beneath the Keurig. "I wan' do it!" Millie cried out.

"Geez, girl, I told you I'm gonna let you do it!" Shiloh replied hoisting Millie to press the button. They stood in silence as the coffee percolated and trickled into the chosen cup decorated with multi-colored hearts.

Millie squealed in delight as the final drops gave way to silence and Shiloh produced the French vanilla coffee creamer from the fridge. Shiloh filled the cup the rest of the way and gave Millie the honors of stirring the two ounces of decaf with the four ounces of creamer.

"Tank to Mama," Millie said with a grin as she stepped down from her stool and brought the cup up to her lips.

"Careful, baby, it may be hot."

"I wan' straw peas."

Shiloh crossed the kitchen to retrieve a straw from another drawer.

"Tank to."

"You're welcome, baby. Be careful not to spill it."

Millie made her way into the living room and set her cup on the coffee table. Shiloh started some cartoons as her older children began to emerge from their bedrooms, carrying everything they had slept with the night before except their mattress, and filled the charcoal-grey couch on the far wall.

"What's for breakfast, Momma?" Ann, her oldest at almost ten years old, asked sleepily.

"There's some donuts on top of the deep freezer," Shiloh offered hoping the idea of sugar laced bread would satisfy her children so she wouldn't have to cook. Ann nodded in agreement and Shiloh returned to the kitchen to fix her own cup of coffee. After replacing the decaf pod with a stronger brew, she hit start and leaned against the wall. She closed her eyes as once again the coffee percolated and trickled, this time into her mug, and the chatter and laughter from the cartoons filled her ears.

Father, forgive me for not tithing my first thoughts to you.

Forgive me for complaining about the kids not sleeping in, Lord, thank you for the blessing of children! Thank you for allowing and entrusting me to be their momma. Grant me wisdom in raising them and guide Harbor and me in all that we do. Help us to remember to parent the kids in a way that's glorifying to You. In Your precious Son, my Savior, Jesus Christ's name, amen.

Coffee in hand, Shiloh retreated to her bedroom to enjoy it along with her Bible reading and devotional time. This was her favorite time of day. She loved spending time with her Lord and drinking coffee, enjoying how her spiritual senses perked-up alongside her physical ones. She drank from the Everlasting Well while simultaneously sipping from her coffee mug, and she'd pray. Oh, how Shiloh cherished her communion with God.

Shiloh had finished her last swallow when Harbor rolled over and pulled her close. She scooted down to lay beside him and snuggled into his embrace. This was Shiloh's second favorite time of the day.

"I'm gonna go for my walk now. You got the kids?" Shiloh asked in a tone that needed no response as she sat Harbor's coffee on the nightstand.

"Uhhh," Harbor groaned in unwilling agreement as he rubbed his face and sat up in bed, reaching over to start in on his morning brew.

Where Shiloh was a morning bird, rising before the sun, Harbor was the night owl and waking up wasn't an easy feat. Shiloh made it less painful though by bringing his coffee and laying out his clothes. Harbor would repay her at nightfall when her eyelids grew heavy long before the children's, handling all the nighttime routines of bathing babies and brushing teeth. Another way God had balanced them out. They operated like a well-oiled seesaw, each taking their turn shouldering the weight of house and home.

"Take your pistol." Harbor found the words somewhere between clearing his throat and sipping his coffee.

"Gah, Harbor, it weighs my pants down," Shiloh protested as she dug in her dresser in search of her favorite faded yoga pants and oversized t-shirt.

"They've found another dead girl in a gully. This one was closer."

"This is Selma, Alabama, Harbor. Stuff like that don't happen here. Besides, I'll have ol' Deputy and Nino." She laughed at her own resolution to the disagreement. Deputy was Harbor's brindle boxer whose arthritis and greying muzzle finally began to match his disposition. Add to that, he was rightly named. Even as a puppy, he didn't play much; rather he laid around like an old deputy, and nowadays, his body mirrored his personality. Nino was Shiloh's overweight pug whose personality resembled that of a spoiled prince: loud but virtually harmless.

Harbor wasn't amused, it was too early.

Shiloh ignored his stare as she dressed and laced up her sneakers. She planted a quick peck on his cheek and escaped out the front door without stirring the suspicions of her children sitting in a television-induced coma.

Outside, she was greeted by the yard bird's squawking and the pig's squealing requests for food. She obeyed and crossed to the small office next door, retrieving scoops of feed and scattering them in the clover field in front of the building. Birdsong and chattering filled the air while bees buzzed underfoot and scents of clover and budding flowers offended her sinuses. Shiloh would pay the price later with a headache, but the sights, sounds, and smells were worth it.

Deputy and Nino had already started their usual trail predicting the route Shiloh would take to their daily spot on the shores of Lake Alayhe. She ran to catch up, exciting them and causing the routine game of catch me if you can. The trio dodged puddles and limbs caused by logging equipment and Shiloh sung hymns and thanksgivings to the Lord.

The sky glowed royal blue speckled with twinkling lights which faded into the background of the rising sun surrounded by streaks of pinks, oranges, and a lighter blue.

Deputy ran off barking his raspy bark chasing a lone spike and Nino just barked, he had done his running for the day. Shiloh wasn't concerned; Deputy would be waiting at their spot, crouched down in an attempt to pick on the fat kid, Nino.

By the time Nino and Shiloh started around the first bend they were met by the elderly groundskeeper, J.B., driving his beat-up multicolored hatchback. He was a peculiar man with a white handlebar mustache and he lived in a camper near the pier and bait shop. Shiloh liked him well enough; he was kind to her family and Harbor favored him.

"Morning!" Shiloh chirped as he slowly passed, mindful of Nino barking at his worn tires. J.B. only nodded.

Winded, Nino left off his harassing and fell into a trot next to Shiloh.

"You told him, didn't you?" Shiloh teased.

Shiloh continued praying for multiple needs of family members and friends, for the leaders in office, and whatever or whoever else came to mind. Sixty-foot pine trees lined the beaten gravel road looking like soldiers at salute, substituting rifles for branches packed with green needles. Voids in the row made the loggers' presence more evident. Lake Alayhe was a tranquil fishing spot but one must be a member of the club for rights to fish it; in order to be a member, you had to hold some type of Doctorate's degree. Shiloh had no desire to take anything from its water, which seemed as if it couldn't decide on whether to imitate the color of the sky above or the trees beside, settling on a brilliant swirled mixture of both.

Closing in on the boat docks, Nino took off barking wildly, the sun in full glory burned Shiloh's eyes. Squinting, she was able to focus in on what Nino started after. A shiny blue pickup with mud trimming the bottom was backing in front of the ramp.

Odd, he doesn't have a boat or trailer...

"Nino!" Shiloh urged, not wanting an aggravated doctor reporting an aggressive pug, denying further permission to walk the grounds without a membership. "Nino! Come! NOW!"

She started towards him to scoop him up and give him a quick pop on the mouth. The closer she got the quicker he became. For a dog who had overindulged in dropped food from small hands he sure could move. Shiloh finally had him within arm's reach and bent over to grab him when she heard a loud crack, then she went deaf and her vision tunneled. She felt the cool ground beneath her, still wet with dew. Her hearing came back slowly, like after shooting her gun, the ringing intensifying until total hearing restored. Nino continued to bark violently, and she'd never heard him so alarmed. Then, her body was snatched off the ground and released, thrown onto the hard feel of metal. She focused her eyes quick enough to see the beautiful sky abruptly eclipsed by the closing of an aluminum toolbox lid.

Shiloh's mind froze from fear and confusion. She pushed on the lid to no avail. Her heart now pounded in her ears and her breathing had quickened. She could still hear Nino barking, but muted. She heard the slam of a vehicle door and the truck jumped forward, thrusting her to the wall of the toolbox. Nino let out a bloodcurdling yelp as she felt something roll violently under the truck. Shiloh's heart sank and she turned new and frightened prayers to God.

ℭℜℽℴ

"Daddy, where's Momma? I'm hungry." Junior asked standing in the bedroom doorway.

Harbor cleared his throat and sat up. Apparently, he had fallen back to sleep with Shiloh out for her walk and the kids quietly watching cartoons in the living room. He glanced at the time on his phone charging on the nightstand. 9:48. Where was Shiloh?

"I don't know, bud, she may be outside." Harbor forced himself out of bed to fix himself another cup of coffee.

"She's not." Nora's voice was as light as her baby blue eyes. She came up behind Junior who looked from Nora to Harbor.

"She's prolly next door working on some invoices." Harbor made his way to the kitchen with the children close on his heels.

"She's not at the office either. I called for her and she didn't answer," Nora replied softly.

"Well, baby, I don't know where she's at. Give me a

minute and I'll call her." Harbor gathered the fixings for his coffee.

"She left her phone." Nora had clearly been searching for her mother for some time but didn't want to wake Harbor.

"I'm hungry," Junior persisted while searching cabinets.

Harbor paused. He glanced at Nora who stood watching him.

"Is Deputy and Nino outside?"

"Deputy is but I haven't seen Nino."

Harbor thought for a moment.

"Her car?"

"It's still outside," Nora replied coolly.

"I'm still hungry," Junior snorted.

"Get you a donut, son," Harbor replied tightly. He sipped his coffee and he made his way back to the room to dress. Nora left off from following him to help Junior fix himself some cereal.

She's been gone since about 6:30. That's almost three hours...

A tinge of panic pricked Harbor's spirit and he dressed faster. He forgot about his coffee and started out the door.

"Where you going?" Ann asked without looking away from the cartoons dancing on the screen.

"I'm gonna drive around the lake real quick and see if I can find your Momma. You're in charge," he replied.

"All right."

"That's not fair!" Junior tried to appeal but Harbor had already closed the door.

With his truck on the path Shiloh was known to take, Harbor thought about all the times Shiloh had asked him to walk with her. He had always replied that he worked all day on his feet and didn't need to add more afterwards.

Now he saw why she loved it. Lake Alayhe was a beautifully scenic area with towering pines and sparkling water. The sounds of birdsong filled the air and the scent of honeysuckle and pine perfumed it.

It didn't take long to reach the bait shop. He parked and went inside, the jingle of an overhead bell alarmed J.B. who came out from the back. Crickets chirping and a drink box which kept can drinks and earthworms cold hummed.

"Heya, Harbor! What can I do ya for?" J.B. limped to the counter with a welcoming smile under his handlebar mustache.

"Hey, J.B., by chance have you seen Shi?" Harbor asked, surprised with how calm he sounded.

"Yeah, I saw her earlier. Prolly around 7-ish. Right before you get to the docks. She ain't made it back yet?" J.B. looked puzzled.

"No." Harbor looked out the windows onto the lake.

"Any fisherman today that might've seen her?"

"Not one today that I know of. S'posed to be storming later." J.B. shook his head.

"Alright. If you see her, tell her I'm looking for her." Harbor sighed.

"I will." J.B. nodded. "You want any help?"

"Uh, nah… Well, actually, yea. If you don't mind, can you finish the loop? I'm gonna go check out the ramp."

"Yeah, man." J.B. started collecting his things as Harbor headed towards his truck for the boat ramp.

Lord, let me find her okay. Let it just be she lost track of time or sprung her ankle or Nino ran off or something.

Harbor circled the boat ramp area and didn't see anything. He parked his truck and got out. He walked to the water and looked around on the ground.

Giving up, he cupped his hands to his mouth and

hollered, *"Sh-i-i-i-i-i-i-i."* Only his echo returned. Again, louder, "Sh-i-i-i-i-i-i-i!"

This time he detected a whimper. Harbor studied the brush, squinting, and saw a black lump underneath a sticker bush. He now could see the trail of blood that led to the pitiful mangled mess of a dog laying there. *Nino?* Harbor knelt down.

"Nino?"

Nothing.

Harbor pulled his limp body from beneath the bushes, numb to the stickers scratching his arms. Harbor studied him. He didn't look mauled. He looked to have been hit, run over. *Shiloh wouldn't have left him like that.*

Harbor wasted no more time. He pulled his phone from the clip on his hip and dialed 911 as he fought waves of nausea.

Two

Jacob pulled into the Pluto Palace parking lot next to Delilah's shiny black mustang. Their vehicles were alone besides a rusted baby blue Taurus with a St. Mary air freshener dangling from the rearview mirror. Jacob eagerly made his way to room number sixteen and rapped it.

Delilah's flirtatious, "Who is it?" caused Jacob's stomach to flutter and his heart to throb. He laughed coolly as Delilah opened the door wearing nothing but a smile.

Jacob had just about dozed off when Delilah's phone rang, its beckoning causing her to abandon his embrace. She dug in her purse a moment before pulling out her cell and a pack of cigarettes.

"Hey, babe. What's up?" She pulled a cigarette from its pack and held it between her lips to light.

The way she answered and fidgeted with her pack of cigarettes, peeling the excess foil left behind during a rush to get to its contents, told Jacob it was her husband, his boss.

"Oh, honey, I'm sorry. Me and the girls got so caught up I forgot to call." She took a long drag as she listened.

Smoke escaped through her nostrils and she blew the remaining out as she ended the call. "Well, I made it and I'll talk to you later. Love you."

She sat at the edge of the bed at Jacob's feet and took a long drag. She exhaled and returned her phone to its designated purse pocket.

Jacob's mind was firing on all pistons as he worked to control his emotions. He didn't want to be alone again. He leaned up and pulled her into his embrace to nuzzle her neck. She held her cigarette out and giggled.

"Jacob…" she started but he didn't want her to finish.

"Marry me," he breathed into her ear and then held his breath as he awaited a response. Her body, which had been soft and pliable to his every touch, had become as rigid as stone. Her answer didn't need to be verbalized; her body language screamed her response.

"Jacob, sweetie…" She took a drag off her cigarette as she pulled away and stood at the foot of the bed.

"Don't ruin this. Aren't we having fun?" she asked with a reassuring and playful smile.

Jacob stared past her as he tried to unscramble his thoughts on her rejection. Did she mean no, or not right now?

"Yeah, but…"

"But what, sweetie? We're gonna live happily ever after?" She rolled her eyes as she teased him.

Jacob's face flashed with heat. "No, I didn't say that."

He remained seated with his legs pulled up and resting his elbows on his knees as Delilah focused on finishing her cigarette, busying herself with gathering her clothes. Jacob found words somewhere between Delilah putting out what little bit of cigarette she had left and her sticking her lighter inside the half-empty pack.

"Why won't you marry me? We've been doing this for over a year now. I'm tired of sharing. I'm tired of tiptoeing around Blann. I'm tired of seeing you lie. Ain't you tired?"

She shot daggers at him from the chair as she tied her sandals.

"Jacob, you can't afford me," she chided.

Silence settled between them, the vein in his throat throbbing as waves of heat flashed across his face. He clenched his teeth and his fists to the point of a headache and bleeding palms.

"I'm gonna get a shower," he snapped snatching the striped covers back. He stomped to the bathroom and slammed the door.

In the tiny stall, Jacob allowed the cold water to run over his face and down his chest, sending a chill that caused goosebumps to emerge on his arms. He was sure the cold water could cool his temper as well as his body, but it only seemed to be working for the latter.

Anger and adrenaline pulsated through him to an unbearable pressure point. It escaped his body through screaming profanities and throwing punches into the wall. He felt no pain; the only indication that he had gone too far was the watered-down blood that swirled underfoot.

Jacob turned off the water and snatched the stark white towel from the shelf fixed above the toilet and dried off. Then he used the rags to wrap his bleeding hands that slowed to a trickle.

"Delilah…" He called for her attention as he snatched the bathroom door open. There was no one there to answer. He looked on the dresser where her bag had been, it now lay bare. He crossed the room in three long strides and pulled open the door in time to see the red glow of her mustang's taillights.

The mixture of fresh cut pine and diesel fuel, along with the clashing of heavy machinery and yelling men caused Jacob's head to pulsate with pain as he climbed out of his rig. He crossed the mangled mess of dismembered branches to the service truck that stayed close by the loader. C.B. radio static and the cracking of falling trees flooded his ears, leaving him deaf to the warning beep-beep-beep of a log skidder backing up.

HHHHHHHOOOOONNNKKKKKK!

The driver in the service truck laid on his horn in an attempt to jolt Jacob back to reality. Jacob cleared a discarded log just in time to watch the skidder's tracks split it into a million toothpicks. Shaken, he observed the claw that dangled midair searching for a stack of logs to snatch up and when it found it's intended target he turned towards the service truck again.

"Man, you better watch out." Todd was manning the truck today. Jacob liked him fair enough. He kept to himself and was a hard worker, knowledgeable in each of the positions that kept the operation running. His only fault was that he claimed to be Christian, which made him the butt of their jokes, and the younger guys took advantage of his "turn the other cheek" mentality.

"Thanks. Didn't sleep good," Jacob said with a shrug as he dug around in the side toolbox of the service truck in search of a Phillips head screwdriver, needed to remove the lens and replace a blown bulb on his trailer. Todd nodded but Jacob sensed he didn't catch what he had said over the noise of the job site. Not eager to risk Todd catching the faint hint of last night's beverages, Jacob focused his energy on ensuring his rig was up to code before hitting the blacktop and risking a trooper being the one to discover his addiction. When Jacob located the screwdriver, he lifted it into the air and nodded with a smile directed towards Todd, who sat watching the loader, alert to answer any calls of distress.

While Jacob cautiously made his way back to his rig to begin his check-over and repairs, he watched as a group of men equipped with only chainsaws, metal cables, and dirty hardhats started towards the marshy land that morphed into the swampy grounds that the machinery wouldn't go. He didn't envy them today as the brush swallowed them effortlessly, the only evidence that they survived was the revving of chainsaws.

Reaching his truck, he went down the checklist and awaited his load. Not too far into it, his truck radio came alive with a squawk.

"Jacob, you copy? Jacob, you copy?" It was the boss. Blann.

Jacob straightened and walked from his trailer to the cab. Climbing in, he grabbed the radio from its holster. "Jacob here. Go ahead."

"Have you gotten loaded yet?"

"Negative."

"Don't. Come to the office, I need to talk to ya."

Jacob hesitated.

"Do you copy? Do. Not. Get. Loaded."

Jacob's stomach flipped and a cold sweat broke out across his forehead trailing his hairline and crawling down his spine. "10-4. I copy."

Minutes later, Jacob pulled into the gravel parking lot and parked near the banner sign with the familiar company logo, *Lot Logging,* as far from the transportable office building as possible. Jacob eyed the other vehicles. Blann

Lot's grey F150 covered in mud sat in its usual spot by the office door, Delilah's, Blann's wife and company secretary, black Mustang sparkled in the sun next to it. The line of muddied trucks and SUVs that sat to the right of the office building and in front of the shop housing various logging equipment belonged to the men who worked alongside Jacob. Nothing looked out of the ordinary.

Jacob was comforted by the crushing of the rocks underfoot as he made his way to the door. He had racked his brain from the job site until he reached the office at what this immediate meeting was concerning. He put a plug of Wintergreen chew in his lip to mask any smell of alcohol that lingered from last night.

He entered the building, Delilah's office sat to the left of the entrance and her door stood open allowing her cigarette smoke to trail into the main hall. Her rat terrier that always sat nestled in her lap or under her feet darted out barking at the sound of Jacob opening the door. He knew the routine, for each Friday he would come in to collect his pay from Delilah, so he stood still waiting for Delilah to command the dog to hush or to come, but she did neither. Had Delilah not been watching, Jacob would've punted the yapping mutt. Delilah rose from her desk and stood in her doorway.

"You ain't scared of her are ya?" She grinned teasingly.

"No, ma'am," Jacob replied.

"What you need, honey?" she asked as she took a drag off her extinguishing cigarette and gave Jacob a quick glance over.

"Uh, Mr. Blann told me to come in." Jacob looked towards Blann's office trying to ignore the obvious look over she gave him.

"Oh, I thought you were coming to see me," she

joked. "Well, he's in there. You know where to go." She nodded towards the door and turned to resume her position at her desk, calling her dog to come.

Jacob smirked and rapped on Blann's door.

"Yeah," Blann called from behind the door.

Jacob opened it and stepped inside. "You wanted to see me?"

"Yeah, close the door and sit down."

Jacob obliged, taking a seat in the worn leather chair that sat catty-corner to Blann's metal desk. Jacob's employee file lay atop forms and a legal pad with numbers scribbled across it.

Blann stared at his computer screen for a few seconds longer and the reflection in his bifocals showed it to be spreadsheets that captured his attention. He closed the tabs and focused his gaze on Jacob.

"How old are you, Jacob?"

"32."

Blann had a look of surprise. "Man, I thought you were older than that." He leaned back into his chair.

"Yeah, I've heard that my whole life," Jacob smirked, relaxing.

Sitting up and crossing his arms on his desk, "You're a grown man and I'm not going to tell you what to do during your off time but when you're on my clock and in my rig, I've gotta. Jacob, you've been a dependable worker since I hired you on. You're a good driver and you show up. That's more than I can say than most of the knot heads I got working here." He opened Jacob's file and again, sat back. "Only complaints I've had on you was back in August and December of last year for smelling of alcohol and you know I can't let you in a truck if you smell of it."

"Yes, sir." Jacob nodded and kept his eyes on his file

while he inwardly cursed Todd. He spit the black colored saliva into his empty soda bottle.

"I got a call on the radio that you almost became a pancake earlier because you weren't paying attention and now that I've got you in here I'm tempted to say I smell a bit of alcohol on you now but I ain't sure, so I won't accuse you." He looked over the rim of his bifocals.

Jacob stared unassuming.

"I'm gonna have to let you sit at home for the rest of the week. At least until we get all the cutting out of the way. Then there'll be less traffic and you won't be so easily distracted."

"I'm good, though." Jacob tried an appeal.

"Naw, let's just wait it out. You ain't fired. I'm just forcing you to go home and get some rest. Come back when you're clear-headed and when the clear cutting is over."

"Yes, sir." Jacob exhaled.

"You can go." Blann dismissed Jacob and immersed himself back into his spreadsheets.

Jacob closed Blann's door behind him and at the sound, Delilah's dog started up again. Jacob crossed the hall heading towards the front door with the little dog close on his heels. Delilah came out of her office.

"Leaving?" she smirked as she slapped her thigh as if to call the dog to obedience.

Jacob nodded, "Yes, ma'am."

"Come on, Fi!" she beckoned for the dog.

Jacob had almost made it to the door when he felt a sting below his calve. He jerked and spun around to see he had been bitten by the dog. Delilah looked as shocked as Jacob.

"That dog just bit me!" Jacob exclaimed as heat flushed his face.

"I can't believe she did that! I'm so sorry! Come in my office and let me clean you up." Delilah knelt down checking the broken skin through the hole in Jacob's worn blue jeans. She swatted at her dog and told her to go lay down. The dog obeyed.

Delilah ushered Jacob into her office and shut the door to keep the dog out. Jacob took a seat near her desk and she hurried gathering a first aid kit and paper towels.

"I'm so sorry. She's never bit anyone before." Delilah's voice seemed sincere with a touch of something else; was it fear? Jacob pondered.

He studied her as she worked on him. She was attractive with her strawberry blonde hair and dressing in a way to which she could show off her tanned skin, but nowhere near the age of Blann. He had to have a good twenty years on her, as she was in her early forties.

She lightly dabbed the bite mark with a paper towel soaked in peroxide before applying some cream and a few butterfly Band-Aids.

"I'm really sorry. You should heal up fine and there's nothing to worry about. Fi is up to date on her shots." She straightened herself and began cleaning up.

Jacob's anger had been subdued with each careful dab her tender hands applied. Jacob stood and went to walk out when Delilah caught him by the arm.

"Hey, what did he want?" she whispered looking Jacob in the eyes.

"What?"

"Blann. What did he want?"

"It was pertaining to business. You're safe." Jacob snatched his arm back and a smile broke out across Delilah's face and she planted a quick peck on his cheek. Her secret was safe.

"Thanks, honey," she chirped as he left her office.

Three

The toolbox smelled of soured beer and motor oil; Shiloh attributed that to the beer cans rattling at her feet and the ratchet straps and tools surrounding her. Tears of frustration and fear soaked Shiloh's hair beneath her head as she laid helpless. Palms bloodied from beating relentlessly on the lid of her metal coffin, her throat raw from cries, and her chest sore from sobbing, Shiloh attempted to pull herself together.

Father! Please. Help. Me!

With balled fists she pounded the lid again and pain shot through her arms like bolts of electricity. She winced from the pain and tried to remember how many turns he had taken.

Left, left, right, left, right, was it another right? Oh, it's no use. I don't even know where we're at. He's been driving for hours. Shiloh's chest was heaving as she cried but no tears would fall.

Father, please. Soften his heart to let me go.

Was God listening? Had He forsaken her?

Make a joyful noise unto the Lord.

Shiloh stopped mid groan.

Make a joyful noise unto the Lord.

It was a soft singsong whisper, like the memory of her children singing in Sunday school.

Shiloh laid still and silently.

Make a joyful noise unto the Lord.

The voice becoming lighter and lighter. Like a fleeting suggestion.

Shiloh tried to make sense of it and began singing an old hymn she had memorized. Her throat burned as though she was expelling fire instead of melodies.

I walk through the garden alone, while the dew is still on the roses

And the voice I hear falling on my ear the Son of God discloses,

And He walks with me and He talks with me

And He tells me I am his own. And the joy we share as we tarry there

None other has ever known.

As the words left her lips, a peace entered her heart and the fear that had paralyzed her and turned her mind to mush no longer pulsated through her veins. Able to focus and searching for an exit, she slowly smoothed her hand over every surface of the cool toolbox that she could reach. Nothing.

Frustration crept in again, blurring her mind's eye at figuring out the formula of escape. She struggled against the sobs that worked to break through. Her eyes stung as her body found more tears to produce.

Make a joyful noise unto the Lord.

The whisper called her attention.

When we walk with the Lord in the light of His word

what a glory He sheds on our way

When we do His good will He abides with us still and with all who will

trust and obey

Trust and obey, for there's no other way to be happy in Jesus than to
trust and obey.

She had heard the hymn and sung it multiple times at their little country church, but the words had never penetrated her hard heart as they did now. She smiled as she sung loudly, and tears of fear became tears of joy. The hum of the motor and the rocking of the truck caused Shiloh's eyelids to grow heavy and without any way to measure time she fell to sleep.

Shiloh jerked awake as the truck came to a stop, banging her head on the lid. Pain and panic washed over her, and her body trembled.

Crrreeaakk.

The toolbox lid opened, and Shiloh looked at a starry sky littered by leaves and branches.

Quickly she searched for the wrench she had felt earlier when she scoped out the toolbox but before she could locate it, she was being pulled up by her ponytail. As he lifted her out of the toolbox and dragged her over the side of the pickup, she tried to remember the self-defense moves she learned in a class at the local gym. Panic plagued her and she thrashed, landing her kicks wherever she could. Some hit the truck, others hit him.

He never said a word while he dragged her behind. She screamed as loud as she could but from the vibrancy of the stars in the night sky above, she was far from civilization. Her screams came back haunting her, reminding her that this was really happening. She was really abducted. All the *Forensic Files* and *Forty-Eight Hours* episodes she had watched never ended with the abductee being found. At least not alive.

The man held her close so she was unable to get any momentum behind her swings and kicks once they reached the crooked door of the run down cabin. He held her in a chokehold as he kicked the door open and she smelled the sweet stench of alcohol. He threw her inside.

Shiloh stumbled over the uneven floor and her eyes struggled to adjust to the one room cabin lit only by an electric lantern. She heard her pulse in her ears as she scrambled to find another exit and then her cries as her attacker's hands yanked the back collar of her shirt.

She turned to face him, kicking him in the stomach with as much power as she could muster. He stumbled back with an exhale. She could see the muddy patterned print the bottom of her Nikes left against his college tee-shirt. Realizing the only way out was through the way she came in, Shiloh lunged for the door. Before she could reach it, his fingers dug into her hips and pulled her to him. She clawed his hands, stomped his steel-toed boots, and tried prying his fingers loose. No good. He had her.

Her attacker pinned her to the floor straddling her under his weight.

"PLEASE! LET ME GO!" she cried.

He did not acknowledge her as he ripped off her shirt. She tried scratching his face, but he deflected and pinned her arms under his knees. The weight of his body on her wrists caused her to cry out. He pulled a foldable knife from his pocket and opened it.

He's going to kill me.

Shiloh tried reasoning with him. "Please! No! Let me go! I won't tell anyone. Please. Just let me go!"

She squeezed her eyes shut and waited to feel the blade glide across her throat. But instead, she felt the dull side of the blade creep between her breast and heard the ripping of fabric as he cut her sports bra. Shiloh's eyes popped open and she stared into his expressionless face. Tears blurred her vision as she realized what she was about to endure.

"I'm going to stand up now. If you move, you're going to regret it. You hear me?"

Shiloh whimpered.

As soon as his weight removed, she scrambled for the door; she would rather be dead than to be forced to give herself to someone other than Harbor.

The man grabbed her by her ankles and twisted. Bolts of pain shot up her leg and she screamed. He took her shoes off as he pulled her back to him. She kicked him in the face and immediately regretted it.

⁞) ⁞

"Why are you wasting time questioning me? Do your job and find my wife!" Harbor snapped at the detective in all black with the name Harris stitched in white across the right side of his chest. Detective Harris loomed a good foot taller and his stocky build granted him an easy fifty-pound advantage. Harbor paid no mind however to the obvious physical superiority; Harbor's hate had proved stronger than worthier opponents in the past.

Harris stood stoic and lifeless, his gaze fixed behind blacked-out sunglasses. Harbor attempted to return his own stare down but the sun glistening off of Harris's bald head left Harbor with a pitiful squint. Frustrated, he let out a groan and slapped the hood of Shiloh's Expedition.

Harris left off scribbling on his notepad to motion a call for calm. "Mr. Romans, this is standard procedure. The

26

quicker you answer these questions the faster I can join my fellow officers on other possible suspects."

Harbor turned, leaning against the hood and he crossed his arms. "Okay," he said in a sigh.

Harris's questions were as the tapping of a telegram, rapid and then a pause, to which Harbor replied igniting the rapid fire of questions again. Questions Harbor had heard detectives asking suspects and eyewitnesses on *Forensic Files.*

"How was ya'll's relationship?" Harris asked, making his way down the mental checklist.

"WAS? It IS fine." Harbor cut his eyes at Harris.

"Were ya'll arguing before she left?"

"No." Harbor stared at the pig and chickens foraging for bugs. His gaze shot upwards at the sound of an airplane. It didn't feel right, the whole world continued to move, to function like nothing was amiss. He wanted to scream. The axis to which his whole world revolved, was missing, leaving him frozen in time. He heard the front door open and at its twice attempt to slam shut he knew it was Millie.

"Daddy, I hungry. I wan cereal." She made her way down the front steps, swatting the dog as he ran up to lick her face.

Harris ceased from his questioning and watched Millie make her way through the yard. She paid no mind to the stranger as she ran up to Harbor slapping him on his thigh.

"Daddy, I wan cc-wc-al!" she demanded with her head cocked to the side. Harris let out a chuckle.

"Tell Sissy to fix you some, baby. I'm talking right now." Harbor nodded back towards the house.

Millie looked curiously at Harris and then with an annoyed grunt at her father she trotted back towards the house hollering for her sister.

"Do you know the route she would've taken?" Harris asked recalling his attention.

"She usually makes the loop around the lake."

"How long does that normally take?"

"About an hour." Harbor shrugged his shoulders.

"Are there any neighbors?"

"No… Well, there's J.B., the groundskeeper. He has an ol' bait shop on the other side of the lake."

"Okay. That's all I need from you for now." Harris produced a card from his shirt pocket. "Here's my info if you think or hear of anything."

Harbor took the card. "Wait. What now?" Panic mixed with urgency distorted his face.

"I'll keep you posted."

"Thanks," Harbor replied, scoffing at Harris's halfhearted attempt at comforting "the husband."

₧₧

Harris made his way to his Tahoe, opened the door but before entering, he looked back at Harbor staring off towards the lake. Many years of solving missing persons cases had thickened his skin, but it also had sharpened his intuition. Harbor was innocent, and Harris did not want to have to come back to tell him that Shiloh was found; dead.

Four

Shiloh looked into the man's grey eyes, cold as steel, sending a chill down her spine and causing her stomach to lurch. "Why me? What did I do?" she asked in between sobs that rattled her chest. She drew her knees up and hugged herself.

"Nothing!" he growled causing her to flinch in fear. "Ya ain't even my type," he spat from across the rotting wood floor as he tossed an empty beer can.

Shiloh pressed her back further and further into the corner of the camp house, pushing so hard she feared she would crash through it. Her mind racing as fast as her heartbeat, fear had her flustered. To calm herself into rational thinking, she dropped her head, resting it on her knees, she began to pray.

Oh, Merciful Father, help me! Help me to get away from this madman! Father please provide an escape! Grant me wisdom Father! Oh, Fath-

The rickety wall finally gave way and let out a loud ripping sound as the weathered boards pulled away from the rusty finishing nails springing back faster than Shiloh could scoot away, pinching her butt causing a painful yelp. Her attacker staggered over and grabbed a handful of her soft brown hair yanking her up by it and causing the sandwich of the wall and floor to take a plug out before releasing.

"AHHHHHH! Let me go you lunatic!" she screeched as she struggled to break his tight grip on her hair. It was no use, she might as well of had her head clamped in an alligator's jaws; his hand was set. Some of her hair ripped free of her scalp and she felt the trickling of blood down the back of her thigh.

The man cursed as he dragged her across the splintery floor and tossed her violently into the opposite corner, spitting when his dip produced too much saliva. Shiloh slammed against the wall and let out a sharp gasp as her head cracked across the floor.

ഇരു

He stumbled over and shoved his finger under her nose, faint breathing. *She lives.* Shiloh was no bother while she lay unconscious, but he wasn't going to let that fool him; she'd only be unconscious a little while longer and the nearest gas station for a beer run was thirty minutes one way.

He pulled back one of the floorboards revealing a cement post with a chain attached to it, driven nearly four feet into the ground. He took the weighty chain and snatched Shiloh's limp left leg, tightly winding the chain three times before securing it with a Master Lock produced from the pocket of his worn blue jeans. Something crimson caught his eye as it glistened down the back of her muscular thigh and he realized what she had hollered for, triggering his explosive anger.

A wave of remorse washed over him as he looked at

the gaping hole left in the bottom of her butt cheek, but that quickly receded as Shiloh groaned and he was reminded of all the groaning he had heard in the past. She may look different but she's just like the rest.

He straightened himself and felt his buzz fleeting, so he waited no longer and left Shiloh naked and unconscious, chained to the floor. As he closed the door, crooked due to the settling of the ground, he bolted the outside and pulled the curtain of kudzu back over it.

As he drove down the deserted drive, swerving to miss potholes and fallen limbs, his mind began to wonder; why did he choose Shiloh? A doe with her fawn jutted across the overgrown path and he slammed on brakes barely missing them. When he reached the end of the rough two-mile pine lined drive he was met with a pair of headlights.

₧₨

Shiloh awakened to the serene company of dustbunnies and empty cans. She spent the next few hours screaming and had screamed every exhale in hopes that a neighbor or a passing car with its windows down would hear her cries for help. Thoughts of hope and efforts became worthless. Her hope died a little with every returned echo. Her hope extinguished more and more until her throat and her persistence burned out.

Shiloh laid on the floor and stared through the hole in the ceiling at the star-studded sky. A million tiny lights twinkled there. How could something so beautiful exist in a world so hideous? She observed the moon full and bright and remembered one Christmas when Ann was a toddler and they had gone to the zoo to see the Christmas lights display. Little Ann squealed with joy as they entered the gates, Shiloh giggled assuming Ann was enamored with the ten-foot sparkling, bulbed teddy bear. Ann ran past the bear, though, with tiny arms outstretched towards the sky where a full, bright moon hung so low even Shiloh thought, for a brief moment, that Ann could reach it.

"Baby, it's just the moon." Shiloh smiled as she scooped her up. Ann continued the rest of the night, "Moon. Moo-moon."

Shiloh pondered, why they focused so much of their attention that night on the artificial feelings the man-made sculptures and displays created, but not on the natural beauty already provided?

Set your mind on things above.

She tried to focus on the words.

Set your mind on things above.

She repeated it again and again until she fell asleep.

Five

"Daddy, I want my Momma," Junior cried and attempted to soothe himself by sucking his thumb.

"I know, baby. I do, too," Harbor whispered and drew him closer.

"I want Momma, too." Millie snuggled into Harbor's side.

Ann and Nora had fallen asleep balled up at the foot of the bed; he had wondered how long it would take them to sleep or if they would at all. Their sleeping faces were swollen and red and the sheets beneath were tear stained. He wanted to cry but would wait until he could do so in private. Even with the children filling his bed up to the point of pushing him to the edge, without Shiloh, it was empty.

೫ಇ

The first week without Shiloh seemed to last a month. Long days of searching and sleepless nights all ran together. Hundreds of their neighbors showed up armed with flashlights and wide eyes. Hundreds more whose knees couldn't bear the terrain, bore the weight of prayer.

Churches held prayer vigils. Family and friends prepared covered dishes which the children and Harbor picked at, but when Shiloh disappeared it was as if their appetite was taken along with her.

The realization that she may never come home became overwhelming when he was informed they were calling off the ground search. Despair crept in and he began questioning to himself was God really good?

"Well, what's next?" He became frantic.

"I'm sorry, Mr. Romans. If you hear of anything, let me know and I'll do the same."

₧₨

Shiloh's eyes stung. Dehydration and days' worth of endless tears left her eyelids swollen and parched, making them act as sandpaper instead of moisturizing wipes with every blink. Her throat burned as she cried out, "Lord, I'm gonna die here, aren't I? Why? Why have you let this happen to me?"

She lay, staring at the rotting ceiling. The air was thick with humidity and the low growl of thunder drew her attention to the hole in the roof. She studied the dark, heavy clouds through the tattered strips of the sun-bleached tarp. A clap of thunder and a flash of lightning made her jump and the pitter patter of rain became louder and louder until the rain coming down was deafening and leaking through the tarp and onto the floor of the cabin. Shiloh hurried to the stream of rainwater and stood beneath it, barely catching swallows due to the smile that parted her lips.

Oh, Father, though I may be dehydrated physically, may I never be dehydrated spiritually. Fill me with the Living Water always!

She stretched her cupped hands up as droplets puddled into her palms and she splashed the water on her face. She shivered as it ran down her chin to her neck and vanished onto her chest.

Thunk. Thunk. Thunk.

The sound of man's index finger striking the can of snuff made Shiloh jump higher than the thunder had earlier.

"Don't stop on my account," he said coolly as he picked a plug of dip from the can and placed it inside his lip.

She stiffened and crossed her arms across her chest. She studied him, the grease on his button-down plaid shirt made her think he was a mechanic, but the scratches and mud that covered his leather work boots said otherwise. He had blown in with the storm, but he wasn't as welcomed as the rain.

"You're back."

"I figured you might be getting lonely."

"I don't think I could ever get lonely enough to enjoy your company," she snapped. He laughed and she walked back to her spot, the sound of her chain dragging the floor contrasting with that of the rain dancing on the roof. Waves of anger swelled within her. "Where do you go when you leave?"

He stared her way.

"Do you have a wife or a mother? A sister or a daughter? How would they feel if they knew I was here?"

His jaw stiffened beneath his salt-and-pepper beard. "It ain't none of your business."

"How would you feel if they were someone's plaything?"

He charged her, stopping right before slamming into

her, causing her to flinch. He squatted down. "You talk too much, you know that?" He breathed into her ear and she jerked away.

"Why don't you just let me go? If you're tired of me let me go!" She stared into his grey eyes.

"Because I'm not done playing." He chuckled as he spit onto the floor beside her and ran his fingertips down her spine. She cowered at his touch and became nauseous.

"Please. Don't. Just leave me here to die." She tried scooting away from him but her grabbed her wrist.

❧☙

Detective Harris rubbed his crossed eyes weary from studying the statements he had scribbled from various people. Shiloh appeared to have been liked well enough. There was no evidence or suspicion of an affair on either side, and no financial woes.

How does a woman vanish into thin air?

He began to rub his temples when his cell rang out. He glanced sideways at the screen where the caller ID read, home. His wife. Probably attempting to submit a last-minute request for something from the store before he headed home. He hit the side button to silence the generic cries that rang out. He closed his eyes and released a long sigh. The tire tracks found and plastered at the scene matched none of the members.

Another dead end.

Hopefully, not another dead body.

He reviewed the autopsy reports of the bodies of the three women found from the surrounding counties. All were blonde and tall. All had been raped. All had been bathed. All had been drowned.

Shiloh didn't fit that description and Lake Alayhe had been dragged, producing nothing but sticks, old tires, and a slew of fishing poles.

හි ලා

Shiloh sat on the dusty floor with her back against the wall, staring at her leg wrapped with the unbreakable chain. She rocked her leg back and forth listening to the clanking the links rang out as they struck together and the thudding sound as the lock rapped the hardwood. Any noise was welcome, filling the eerie silence that seemed to be driving her mad, even the song of captivity the chains sang. Shiloh struck the floor with balled fists and let out an aggravated groan.

"GOD! I CANNOT DO THIS ANY LONGER! HE'S NOT GOING TO CHANGE!"

Please, please, please, let me break free somehow.

Tears of frustration puddled in her eyes and the ones that ran left pale streaks of clean skin down her cheeks as the waters of depression began to drown her. Her spirit fought against her circumstances, trying desperately to medicate the broken parts with songs of praises and thanksgiving but none would come out. She had lost count of the days but knew it had been long enough that the medications she used to control her depression had been flushed from her system.

She rose from the floor and stretched her body enough so her fingertips could touch the seal of the broken window, outside wasn't much to see, overgrown kudzu and entwined tree limbs blocked most of the view except for a small opening if she turned her head just so.

Beyond the brush and briars laid a small creek bed

which explained the trickling of water Shiloh had heard after a rainstorm. An abandoned green plot planted by hunters years ago still produced a lush bed of vibrant green grass. Shiloh couldn't tell if she gasped at the beauty or at the stab of pain that shot up her leg as the chain resisted closer investigation, reminding her where she was imprisoned.

Shiloh walked the path she had made in the dust as she imagined escaping scenarios.

I'll pluck a shard of glass from the broken window and when he tries again, I'll kill him. Then I can get the key and get out of this living hell. But what if he overpowers me? He'll kill me for sure. I'll wait, maybe he'll pass out and then I'll have the element of surprise on my side.

Pray for your enemies, love those who persecute you.

The voice made Shiloh stop in her tracks, refusing, she shook her head and continued pacing and plotting.

I can act like I want him. Maybe that'll turn him off and he'll let me go. She shuddered at the thought. She wasn't some sexy heroine in a comic book. She wasn't a very good liar either so acting wouldn't prove productive.

Pray for your enemies, love those who persecute you.

She shook her head again as anger choked her.

Pray for your enemies, love those who persecute you.

"I'm not you. I can't." Shiloh's face grew hot and her nails dug into her palms as she held tight fists.

Pray for your enemies, love those who persecute you.

"I won't."

"You won't what?" He closed the door behind him startling Shiloh. Had she been so distracted that she didn't hear his truck pull up? His clothes weren't his usual worn t-shirts and faded blue jeans which emptied into cracked leather work boots, today he donned khaki slacks which brushed the top of brown dress shoes and a plaid button up with sleeves he had rolled three quarters of the way up his arm. He looked like a normal middle-aged guy headed to Sunday night service, unsuspecting, except for the cool grey of his eyes which hinted at his coldness.

Shiloh immediately sank back down covering herself up as best she could by hiding in the shadows.

"You won't what?" he asked again peering through the darkness at her as he pulled his can of dip from his shirt pocket and stuck a plug in his lip.

"Lie," Shiloh snapped back.

He chuckled, "That's impossible, you're a woman."

Shiloh stared at him with a face blank of expression and shrugged her shoulders as if to tell him it made no difference what he thought.

"Alright. How'd you get all them stretch marks? You got any kids?" He sat leaning against the table crossing his hairy arms across his chest as he adjusted his plug of tobacco with his tongue.

Shiloh's ears rang as blood rushed to her head and her pulse quickened. She wondered if she had let something slip in her sleep. Did her body harden at the mention of his observance and had he noticed?

Lean not unto thine own understanding.

The voice was so faint she had barely heard it, much less understood.

"Well?" His patience waned.

Shiloh cleared her throat. "No." She shook her head and rolled her eyes looking away from him and fixing her eyes on the pile of discarded cans as she hugged her knees.

He snorted in disbelief as he started towards her.

Shiloh stiffened and stared him straight in the eyes, she wanted him to see her hate. He leaned down and snatched her left leg, pulling her towards him. She began to kick and swing at him.

"No," he hissed through clenched jaws as he smacked her hands and legs.

Shiloh continued fighting, she wasn't going to let him have her without a fight.

"I'm taking you to get a bath," he snapped as he slapped her face hard.

Shiloh sat still as he pulled his key chains etched with the name *Jacob* from his pocket unlocking the lock and, to Shiloh's surprise, carefully unwrapped the chain from her leg.

Shiloh glared at the raw pink flesh and gagged at the decaying scent that rose from it.

"Come on." He held a tight grip on her arm and pulled her to her feet, chauffeuring her to the door.

The sun, no longer filtered through leaves and dust or blocked from rotting walls, blinded Shiloh's eyes and clouded her mind. The sun was a welcoming warmth on her bare skin and the crushing of leaves underfoot was comforting. The earthy smell of the dirt and the trickling of the creek reminded her of her favored times of prayer while jogging around Lake Alayhe.

The few yards they had walked proved to Shiloh just how weak her body had become. The mere thought of attempting an escape winded her.

Briars scraped across the tops of her feet and tugged at her ankles as she limped alongside him. He was taller than Harbor and every bit as strong, as he led her to the creek where he had already set up toiletries and a towel hung from a tree limb hanging nearby.

A flash of red caught her eye as she made her way onto the cool creek bed. A small red rose bush with four blooms grew up beneath a bush. The roses reminded Shiloh of Harbor. Last year in the depths of a depressive episode Shiloh felt as though her marriage to Harbor was deteriorating as she fought against depression's drowning waters. Each disagreement seemed monumental and Shiloh, usually a fighter, began to shut down. Lies flooded her mind and she believed that Harbor no longer loved her. During one of their heaviest fights Shiloh explained to Harbor, "My love for you is like a flower. It will not leave. It's rooted. But it's up to you to water it and watch it flourish or neglect it and watch it wither."

The next day after a sleepless night of avoiding touching one another, Shiloh had been tending to children when a knock on the door startled the dogs and kids throwing everybody into a frenzy. She calmed everyone down best she could and answered the door.

A dozen red roses and a handwritten card from Harbor that read, "I want to see you bloom."

Shiloh wanted to smell the flowers. She wanted to feel that love again. She wanted to be home to calm her chaos down.

"Get in." He pushed her into the water.

She stumbled in and the icy water stung her open sore making her gasp.

"Lie down."

She looked at him as if he had two heads growing out his neck.

"Don't look at me like that. Lie down."

She refused.

"You don't want me to come in there."

She stared past him. If he wouldn't let her free, she was going to make it Hell for him to keep her.

He rushed her and she moved past him, pushing him into the creek bed. Realizing too late what she had done, she didn't make it all the way out of the water before he had her by her hair pulling her back in.

<h1 style="text-align:center;">Six</h1>

Sunrise came before sufficient rest for the day ahead was achieved.

"I wan offee!" Millie, after ten minutes of asking, now screamed her demands in an attempt to motivate a groggy-eyed Harbor.

"Millie, NO!" Harbor snapped, resisting Millie's tug on his floral-patterned blanket.

Millie threw her small body into the floor with a grand thud which shook Harbor's bed.

Harbor threw his covers back and sat up, blindingly searched for his slippers while spatting off warnings to the tiny terrorist who lay at his feet flopping about. She hopped up as fast as she fell down and followed him into the kitchen to retrieve her coffee creamer with a dash of decaf. Harbor pushed the sacred start button on the Keurig in ignorance, triggering another melt down.

"Millie! What is wrong with you?! I'm fixing your coffee!" Harbor's eyes which were once blinded with sleep now replaced with rage.

Junior entered the kitchen whining and covering his ears due to the screeching of his little sister.

"Daddy, make her hush," Junior pleaded.

"I'm trying!" Harbor snapped as he snatched the coffee cup off the counter and placed it on the dinner table in the dining room adjacent.

Millie now stood, pumping her tiny, yet powerful legs into a repetitious stomp as she cried for a bendy straw to drink her coffee.

The phone began ringing from Harbor's nightstand and in a rush to answer its generic bidding, his vision failed him at noticing a misplaced neon pink tennis shoe catapulting him forward and causing a head-on collision with the door jam.

"Dang it! Girls! Get in here and pick your stuff up!" he howled as he rubbed the corner of his eye. He slammed his bedroom door to stifle the fiasco still unfolding. He attempted to calm his voice to answer the phone in a likable, customer service tone.

"Romans Ready Mix." Harbor tried to sound the complete opposite of how he actually felt.

The voice on the other end was unfamiliar yet comforting.

"Oh…I'm sorry…I must've gotten the wrong number. I'm looking for Shiloh."

Harbor had to clear his voice before answering. "No, you've got the right number. She's gone, though…Maybe I can help you?"

The silence on the other line and the silence from the dining room made him unnerved, he crept back to his door and opened it slowly as if he was opening the door to a ferocious lion's cage. He peeked around the corner to see Millie sitting happily atop the table slurping her coffee through a straw that Junior provided.

"Well… I had heard she was missing and I had to see for myself."

Harbor wanted to scream into the phone that his wife's disappearance wasn't some episode of *Forty-Eight Hours* or *Cold Case Files* to be gawked at by viewers who delight in gloom and doom. This was his life and his wife!

"Is that all?"

"No, I'm sorry. That sounded horrible. That's not what I meant." The warm, peaceful voice's sincerity could be felt through the phone line.

"It's okay…What can I help you with?" Harbor felt at ease with the young lady's voice.

"Actually, I was calling to see what I could help you with?"

Millie had run out of coffee so she dismounted the table and headed towards her older sister's room and once inside, shrieked out new cries.

"Nothing. Just prayers." Harbor had more than enough practice in this exchange. Shiloh had been gone for weeks and phone calls had slowed to a trickle, but the words were always the same.

"It sounds like you need more than just prayers," she chuckled overhearing the ruckus in the background.

"Who is this?!" Harbor was not amused.

"Oh, I'm sorry! I'm Emily Sisters, I met Shiloh at a spiritual retreat last year."

ഇൽ

Shiloh heard the all too familiar hum of Jacob's truck long before it ever made it to the abandoned cabin and her makeshift prison.

Father, I loathe it here. Please let him turn me loose soon. I miss Harbor and the babies. I miss my church family. I miss my Bible. Father, please let me not forget Your Word, Lord. Thank you for the bird that sat on the roof and sung me a song this morning. It lifted my spirit, Lord! You haven't forgotten me; you always show your strength in my weakness and I praise you, Lord!

Pray for your enemies, love those who persecute you.

Shiloh's head shot up as she heard the words as clear as if they'd been whispered directly into her ear. She glanced around the sunlit streaked room only to find the same company of discarded beer cans and floating dust particles. How she wished she could be as the dust, virtually invisible unless the sun hit it just right; she longed to be free. Why had Jacob chosen her? He even said it himself, she wasn't his type. Whenever he forced himself on her it seemed as if he loathed it; loathed her. Shiloh had been molested as a young teen by two different boys and though she hated it as much as she hated Jacob's attacks, she didn't feel such hate permeating from their unwanted touching.

Since marrying Harbor and becoming a Christian, Shiloh made sure her dress was modest. She knew how her tiny waist gave way to wide hips and thick thighs, catching the eyes of nearly every man she encountered. Betting that they were waiting to catch a glimpse of her butt as she passed would be cheating, like peeking at the cards in another's hand: it was a given.

Every morning she would ask Harbor, "is this modest?" before heading out the door and into the public eye. At first when the conviction of her dress hit, Harbor hated it. He was proud of the beauty his wife held and he trophied her; when one has a trophy what good is it if no one knows? Over time, Harbor grew to appreciate his wife's newfound modesty. It gave her an innocence he had never seen in her, leading him to love her tenderly and more intimately. Their love which had started out as an engulfing bonfire, destined to burn out fast just as extremely hot fires do, grew into the steady glow of a hearth log surviving even the coldest nights of their marriage. Better to simmer in love than to burn in lust.

Shiloh thought over her outfit that she had worn that early Spring morning at Lake Alayhe. She had been so careful, making sure her oversized t-shirt fell well below her shapely behind and she fed her muscular legs into a faded black, well-worn pair of loose fitting yoga pants that were three inches too long and dragged the ground. Dingy sneakers and a messy bun atop her head and a face bare of makeup. It wasn't the way she was dressed that invoked her abduction. Why had he chosen her?

The slamming of Jacob's truck door caused Shiloh's stomach to rise into her throat, if she had eaten lately, she was sure it would have wasted all over the creaky wooden floorboards. It had been so long since she had eaten, the hunger pains in her stomach now dulled.

Father, please, please let today be the day. Please let him be tired of me. Please let me go home to my husband and babies.

Jacob stooping, entered the cabin with two armfuls of brown grocery bags, dropping them on the table made up of two rugged, paint splattered sawhorses overlaid with a sheet of warped plywood that sat just inside the door. Shiloh watched him with curiosity as he emptied the contents of the first paper bag; a pack of baby wipes, a gallon of water, a couple of cans of potted meat, and a sleeve of saltine crackers.

Oh, Father! He doesn't plan on ever turning me loose! I won't eat Father, I'll starve to death before I stay here with this terrible man!

My strength is sufficient for you.

I know it is but Father please! Strike him dead so I can escape!

Pray for your enemies, love those who persecute you.

The second bag held two twelve packs of canned Bud Light. Jacob tore the cut out cardboard handle and pulled out a beer, peeling back the tab and producing a crisp pop that reverberated off the walls. He used his tongue to push the plug of tobacco out of his lip and spat it on the floor. He lifted the can to his lips and took a long drink before lowering it with a satisfied sigh. Grabbing a can of potted meat and the sleeve of crackers he tossed it at Shiloh.

"Eat."

Shiloh glared at him.

Pray for your enemies, love those who persecute you.

She wanted to ignore the stirring of her spirit. She wanted to neglect the request of God and write it off as if she hadn't heard Him. She wanted vengeance. She wanted Jacob struck down and she wanted to witness it.

Pray for your enemies, love those who persecute you.

God was yelling it into her heart. His words filled the small dimly lit room almost crushing her. Shiloh bowed in obedience and fear, taking the potted meat and crackers she blessed them. *"Merciful Father, thank You for Your provisions and I pray that this food will nourish my body for Your service, here on this Earth. Forgiving Father, I pray for Jacob, let Your Will and not my own be done."* Shiloh raised her head and peeled back the lid on the can and tore open the plastic wrapper of the crackers and began to eat.

Jacob stared at her in disbelief and disgust. Shaking his head, he threw the empty can into the floor and once again, reached into the cardboard box pulling out another bold blue can.

"Why did you choose me?" Shiloh asked in between bites.

Tipping his chin back to allow a freer flow of the

golden elixir he took a long drink before answering.

"I've done told you. I don't even know," he answered through clenched teeth. The other women never asked why, they never asked anything except would he kill them. This one proved to be as bad as a toddler going through the infamous why stage. Clearly, she had never outgrown it.

"I think I know why," Shiloh said matter-of-factly. Shiloh's mouth watered at the gas station lunch special, but it didn't produce enough saliva to choke down the stale saltine crackers. She eyed the gallon of water.

Jacob continued the rhythmic motion of tipping his head back, long drink, until the can emptied and like a well-oiled machine, started again with a new can.

Shiloh knew she had about twenty more minutes before Jacob would make it through half of the first case and the effects start kicking in. She knew how to time it and when to be quiet, she had grown up in a family with two alcoholic parents.

"How many women were there before me and how many will there be after me?"

Jacob cut his eyes at her and hesitated before answering, he knew he needed to word it in a way that would strike fear to her very core.

"I've lost count and I don't intend on trying to keep up with it." He smirked a sinister smile surely painted by the Devil himself as he slammed the gallon of water in front of her before strolling across the room back to his perch beside his beer.

"Aren't you tired? Always hungry, always feasting, but never full." Shiloh could feel God softening her heart for her attacker. She studied his worn face and saw a brief painful flinching of his eyes, had she blinked she would have missed it.

Jacob snatched the pack of baby wipes from the table but dropped them, though Shiloh was still chained he never turned his back on a pig, he kicked the wipes and they flipped and slid into Shiloh's dirty feet.

"Wipe yourself off, you smell like a pig." He growled and he started on his fourth can.

"I think I know why I'm here. Satan wants you to destroy me, but God wants to save you."

Her abductor had no reply.

<h1 style="text-align:center">Seven</h1>

Shiloh took the wipes, opening them slowly and tearing the inner seal causing the fragrance of aloe and Shea butter to burst in her nostrils triggering tender memories of her babies. Ann was almost ten and turning into a fine young lady, spitting image of Shiloh except for the smile and dimples she inherited from Harbor, well versed in the Scriptures and could hold a steady theological conversation. Nora had just turned seven, she was a vision of beauty herself though she looked nothing like her mother; platinum blonde ringlets framed her porcelain skin and thick long eyelashes surrounded sky blue eyes, she was shy and quiet but quite the observer since infancy. Junior was almost four and named after his Daddy and rightly so, he was the carbon copy of Harbor except for the coarse sandy blonde hair that seemed to grow up instead of long and he had doe eyes just like his Momma. Millie was a firecracker despite her tiny stature, though she was well past one she could still fit into twelve-month clothes.

Dynamite comes in small packages…

Harbor and Shiloh would jokingly say that Millie was God's way of humbling them for the pride they held in the older, well behaved children. Shiloh could see her little firecracker running lopsided across their lush green yard; nothing on but her diaper and a smile, her hair and eyes the same coloring as Nora's but instead of ringlets, her locks were pin straight and swayed effortlessly in the wind. She'd stop long enough to push her bangs that lay flat across her forehead out of her eyes and pick a dandelion to bring to her Momma.

"Bow, Mama." Millie would toddle back to her, arm extended holding the daffodil out to Shiloh for her to blow the seeds into the sky. Shiloh would smile and oblige to her spunky toddler with the rosy cheeks and contagious smile.

Oh, she missed her babies, her husband, her home. She missed how all of them, though there was a variety of species ranging from fowl to canine to pig, lived in harmony. She likened it to what Heaven must have been like before the Fall.

Shiloh wondered how her family was coping without her; did Harbor make the girls' sandwiches for lunch the way they liked it? Ann liked mayo but despised mustard and Nora was just the opposite. Did Junior need his nails clipped? He was prone to scratching himself in his sleep in the process of sucking his thumb. Was Millie running around bare butt?! Harbor had never changed a diaper and Millie wasn't yet potty trained. Imagining Harbor gagging over Millie's diaper blowout caused Shiloh to giggle.

"WIPE DOWN NOW!" Jacob hollered interrupting her fantasy of home.

Shiloh obeyed and began wiping at her feet blackened with God only knew what and worked her way up her legs; mosquitos had clearly enjoyed her. She grimaced as she tediously wiped the raw, pink flesh surrounding the chain. She was careful to keep her legs pulled in covering her bare torso and her feet crossed over her private areas. She wanted to give him no satisfaction; he wasn't interested in her, right now all of his attention was held by the half empty case and nightmares that haunted him even during the day.

Shiloh slipped back into her fantasy world as she wiped her armpits.

How was Nino, Shiloh's black blob of a Pug, was he even alive after that dreadful day at Lake Alayhe? She hoped so. He had helped her through some of her darkest days. Harbor had bought him for Shiloh after her bout with postpartum depression following Millie's birth; it left Shiloh and Harbor fearful of another pregnancy and eventually led to Harbor's vasectomy. Nino filled Shiloh's empty lap when squirmy toddlers abandoned it for adventures unknown.

Harbor…how was his heart? Had it grown cold to the promises of the goodness and mercy given by God? Where Harbor could talk sensibly to Shiloh, easing her anxiety of worldly concerns that seemed to plague her regularly; Shiloh breathed faith into his heart when things were out of his control. She could see his knowing green eyes and grin. She could feel his callused hands as they turned soft as silk caressing her shoulders. For a brief moment she thought she caught a whiff of his scent; clean soap smell with hints of his woodsy cologne she had bought him for Christmas from Bath & Body Works. Had Harbor slept at all? He never could sleep without Shiloh next to him. After each child's delivery, when night fell, Harbor would decline the offer of a cot for the cramped hospital bed Shiloh would share with him. It was cramped, but he could sleep for she fit perfectly into the crook of his body. The nurses at the nurse's station commented once on how it made them uncomfortable walking in to find them spooning in the single person bed, Harbor replied nonchalantly, "If that makes you uncomfortable then you don't want to know what we did to make it in here." Shiloh couldn't tell whose cheeks blushed faster or redder, hers or the middle-aged nurse's.

The crashing of a tossed beer can against the other empties jolted Shiloh back into reality. She had unknowingly used six wipes to finish her clean up and staring into the once white wipes with little imprints of alphabet blocks now discolored with markings of black, brown, and the dull reddish brown color of dried blood; she tried to count how many days she had been there.

Jacob had polished off the second case and the effects were in full swing. She had hoped he would have forgotten her.

He hadn't.

Jacob's steel grey eyes seemed to have turned black as he peered at Shiloh and while making his way to her, he began unbuckling his belt.

Shiloh bowed her head and began praying.

Fear and anger blinded Shiloh as she curled up in her dirty corner of the cabin. She had stumbled across many abandoned houses and cabins when hiking, curiosity leading her to investigate them and imagining the families that had lived in them before. Now she wondered how many had been someone else's prison.

She kept her eyes shut tight as the crisp sound of a can's tab peeled open and the exhale of its contents filled her ears. Jacob was drinking himself into oblivion as he always did after an attack.

If he can't stand it, then why does he do it?

She wanted to ask him, why? Why do you hurt me which causes you to hurt yourself with the drinking?

Shiloh had experience with alcoholics, her parents both struggled with the bottle. She was the second of five children born to two poor, addiction-ridden parents. Shiloh grew up all over Central Alabama, moving often due to her dad's ever-changing professions as he got fired from every job due to his substance and alcohol abuse, and inability to keep the rent paid. Yet she grew up relatively happy, considering her circumstances. Her parents tried their best, but the insatiable appetite for the "party life" possessed them, they couldn't appease it, and the influential group that seemingly surrounded her family like a dense fog wasn't very positive, especially not towards the idea of a white picket fence kind of lifestyle.

No, for Shiloh it was broken-down single-wide trailers or eerily irreparable 1800s-era homes in the "bad" part of town. Growing up though she could remember many times thinking that this was not how life was supposed to be. Not that she really had examples from anywhere else since she didn't start staying the night over at friends until 2nd grade or so, but from what she saw on T.V., families were all smiles, and so much affection, big houses, nice cars, church goers, pure bred dogs, the works.

Shiloh's family paled in comparison to T.V. families. She and her siblings basically raised themselves as far as moral standards, not that her parents didn't try. She could still see her father's red eyes and sunken look, shoulders slumped due to another lost daily battle against the bottle, she could smell the sickeningly sweet aroma of alcohol mixed with the musk of his latest joint.

"Don't be like me," he pleaded with them.

They didn't want to be, none of them did, they all

wanted out and yearned for escape moment by moment.

Shiloh's momma was present, but she either sat quietly drowning herself in her bottle or was shouting disapprovingly at Daddy for the exact same thing she was doing herself. It was a vicious, finger-pointing cycle closely resembling a scene where two people are in a sinking boat, both rocking and flailing about causing the boat to sink faster, and unfortunately, there were no bystanders to throw a life-preserver.

Years of anguish at home turned Shiloh bitter, anxious, and angry. A desire to inflict those same emotions on any authority she faced consumed her. Never tying up with any other students, adults were her target. Future seems grim for children such as Shiloh and her siblings. They should have followed their parents' examples, statistically speaking, only by the grace of God, they hadn't. Shiloh had had her equal share of stumbling and screwing up but thought she turned out okay.

The sound of choking pulled Shiloh from her memory. She cracked an eyelid to peek at what the noise was about. She made out the outline of Jacob, passed out, lying flat on the floor with a beer still in his hand. She studied him for a moment. Choking, his chin jerked up while his eyes stayed shut.

Help him, a whisper in the air demanded.

Shiloh sat up. She looked around but there was no one.

I'll wait, she thought, *maybe he'll wake himself up…or die.* A sensation of satisfaction and relief crawled down her spine with the latter thought.

Jacob let out a choking sound again, this time louder. He wasn't going to wake up.

Help him.

Her conscience prodded her. Pushing her into submission.

I can't. He has hurt me. He has hurt others. He deserves to choke to death. She shook her head as she pulled back for control.

Seventy times seven.

No!

Seventy times seven.

Jacob grew quiet and still as a bubbling stream of bile escaped the corner of his lip, spilling onto his cheek and onto the floor.

Shiloh scurried across the floor on all fours but just before reaching him, her chain snatched her back. A jolt of pain shot up her thigh and into her hip. She inhaled sharply through clenched teeth.

She reached as far as she could, leaving her chain leg suspended in the air as she crawled her fingers towards Jacob. She was able to pinch the hem of the sleeve of his shirt. She pulled but it slipped from her grasp.

God, if you want me to do this, you've gotta give me the ability!

'Hey!" Shiloh yelled. "HEEEEEYYYYYY!"

Jacob didn't respond.

Shiloh rested on her heels as she scanned the room. With no other options, she began pelting Jacob with discarded beer cans.

Movement. Jacob's eyes fluttered and he began choking again.

Shiloh continued hitting Jacob with cans and hollering until he awoke.

"Quit it," Jacob slurred as the remaining vomit poured out of his mouth and he mean-mugged Shiloh.

"You mean, thank you," she snapped as she crawled back to her corner, creating as much space as possible between them.

Jacob stared at her in confusion as he sat up and leaned against the wall and rested his elbows on his knees.

"You almost suffocated on your vomit," Shiloh answered his confusion.

Shiloh woke to an empty cabin and wondered how long it would be before he would return. The hours seemed as minutes when she heard the gravel of the drive crunching beneath a truck's tires.

"Here." Jacob tossed a bundle of fabric to Shiloh who sat in her usual corner of the cabin.

She watched as it made a soft thud at her feet. "What is it?" she asked as she began to unravel it. Jacob ignored her question and began to tear open his usual pack of aluminum confidence. After unwrapping a white hotel comforter and sheets, she held up a men's green and navy plaid button down. Thankfulness welled up inside her as she blinked back tears.

"Thank you," she whispered as she slipped her arms into the sleeves, she imagined that the shirt that fit more like a dress on her, provoked the same emotions in her as it did a poverty stricken child in a third world country receiving a Samaritan's Shoebox filled with necessities and goodies at Christmas.

Jacob, once again, ignored her.

She busied herself with creating a pallet with the down comforter and various sheets. Funny, how she had once complained on sleeping on anything other than her memory foam mattress and now she felt more like a queen atop her pallet made of cracker wrappers for cushioning and folded up sheets.

Eight

"It's been over two months. The flyers on the local businesses' doors have begun to fade. Is there anything more we can do?"

Harris searched for the answer on the ceiling of his office as he laid back in his chair. He rubbed his head before answering.

"We can try a press release."

"Anything is better than nothing. I can't stand doing nothing."

"Yeah, I understand. I'll see if I can get something set up and call you."

"Alright, thanks, man."

"Yes, sir."

Harris hung up his phone and began to look up the local news station's number.

ഈ

"Daddy, I wan' seep witch you," Junior managed to say while sleepily sucking his thumb.

"Not tonight, buddy." Harbor replied drawing his son into his arms to carry him to his own bed. Junior managed to muster up a whine for argument's sake as they entered his navy-blue room, but Harbor laid him down gently and covered him with his comforter patterned with heavy equipment and work trucks.

"Night, son." Harbor leaned down to plant a quick peck on Junior's smooth cheek.

Junior's eyes popped open and he yanked his thumb out of his mouth. "Sing me a song?" Junior's eyes pleaded.

Harbor straightened as his heart sank onto the construction zone rug. Shiloh had sung a lullaby she had made to each of the babies whenever they couldn't sleep, the older two had grown out of needing their Momma's singing to soothe them but the younger two were still in that stage.

"Baby, I can't sing."

"Pwease."

"Son, I can't. I don't know how it goes."

"Sleepy baby, sleepy baby, goodnight sleep tight. Sleepy baby, sleepy baby…" Harbor jerked around as the lullaby came from the hallway behind him, Ann stepped into the dimly lit room singing her mother's song and executing it beautifully.

Junior resumed sucking his thumb as Ann continued singing and snuggled into bed next to him.

"Good night, I love ya'll." Harbor nodded at them as he headed back down the hall.

He peeked in on Nora lying in bed and studying the pictures in a fairy book and paused at Millie's door, placing his ear to it and held his breath. Silence. Satisfied that everyone was settled in for the night he made his way through the living room littered with abandoned toys to the master bedroom.

He stood in the doorway looking in at the bed he

shared with Shiloh for twelve years, his eyes fixed on her side where she would be sleeping or waiting for him to return, depending on how hard the day proved. Now it was empty.

God… Harbor attempted to pray but words wouldn't form.

He stood staring until his eyes stung and his ears could no longer hear the distant lull of his oldest daughter's voice. He climbed into bed and turned on the T.V. to distract himself from the deafening silence and to fill the emptiness with colorful characters that flashed across the screen. The ghost of Shiloh's presence wouldn't permit Harbor to focus on the storyline that played out before his eyes. He turned over, facing her side and wished he could pull her into him as he had done so many nights before, settling for her pillow, he buried his face into it and breathed in her scent that still lingered. Visions of Shiloh danced in his mind until they too, vanished just as his wife had, giving way to darkness.

Harbor jolted as he felt his body falling off the bed. Without Shiloh lying next to him acting as a guardrail, in his sleep Harbor had managed to toss and turn from his side, pass Shiloh's and onto the floor. Grumbling, he rose and picked up the blanket and pillows that accompanied him during his avalanche and tossed them back onto the bed.

He situated himself into the middle of the bed and surrounded himself with pillow barricades. The T.V. had timed itself out so the only light came from the soft glow of the digital alarm clock that read 2:32 a.m. Harbor closed his eyes and tried to pick up the prayer that he had left off earlier.

God…

Harbor's heart weighed so heavy already that the name of God seemed to be a weight he couldn't bear.

God…

Harbor wrestled with his mind trying to find the words, until his heart blurted them.

God, help me.

Harbor repeated that prayer until he drifted back to sleep.

"Shi!" Harbor hollered out across the chalky white dust-covered work yard, his aggravation seeming to rise along with the sun. Orders were to be typed and trucks needed to be batched with pungent-smelling concrete destined to become sturdy foundations for future houses and driveways but his batch women, who happened to also be his wife, was not in her dutiful position inside the 12'x12' block batch house that held the admixtures, digital scales, computer for typing said orders, carcasses of long deceased insects along with forgotten spun webs, and metal desk littered with voided orders, company pens, and whatever else the eight employees who frequented the business' hub decided to thoughtlessly toss onto it.

"Dang it! Where is that woman!" he muttered under his breath as he crossed the dust covered concrete yard in the direction of the twenty-year-old doublewide trailer he shared with his wife and four children. The assorted breeds of nine chickens and black and white potbelly pig flocking to him in hopes of being fed.

"Ya'll get on now!" He swatted and kicked at them in frustration. "Heck of a note I ain't even gotta ask for ya'll and ya'll come running."

Before he made it within ten feet of his desired destination, he heard the creaking of the front door and a familiar petite silhouette appeared in the doorway of his home.

"I'M COMING! I'm only one person, Harbor…" Shiloh shuffled down the steps while slipping her arms into her lightweight coral colored sweater and alternating her granola breakfast bar in her hands. She scurried by, slowing down just a moment so he could catch her cutting eyes at him.

"Don't start with that. I told you last night we had to start early this morning. They want mud on the job at 7:00." Harbor fell in line behind Shiloh as they headed to the batch house and smirked as she too swatted at the herd of animals vying for her attention.

"I'm not starting anything. I had to get the kids up, fed, and motivated to get dressed and then I had to get their lunches packed." She felt his eyes boring holes into the back of her head; she didn't care. They'd been together and business partners long enough they both knew that this morning was no different than any other morning and would most surely not be the last of cutting eyes, frustration, and rushing.

Shiloh slung open the heavy metal door and stepped up into the batch house greeted by her employee's warning calls of "boss lady" in an attempt to hush any crude talk. She made her way through the crowd of matching uniformed drivers and took her place in front of the computer screen and batch control board; tuning out the commotion behind her as Harbor explained in great detail the directions to the various jobs the drivers would be delivering to.

She was so focused on typing out all the correct information on the tickets she didn't even hear them leave out to get into their trucks. Harbor engulfed her in his arms from behind and nuzzled his face into the nook of her neck causing goosebumps to break out down her slender arms. Shiloh struggled to break free from his hold.

"Stop it! Someone is going to see us!"

"Who?! A couple of dead flies?!" Harbor retorted as he lifted his head from the sweet scent of her neck; he loved the way she always smelled of coconut and vanilla, except for when she went for her daily jog around Lake Alayhe, he hated the way she smelt after her therapeutic hike; a mixture of pine, stagnant water, and sweat.

"Now you know good and well one of the guys could come waltzing back in here at any given moment." Shiloh managed to twist out of his hold and now turned looking up into Harbor's bright green eyes and his Cheshire Cat grin; Harbor was voted biggest flirt and best smile in High School and rightly so, he had unbelievable charm that got him out of trouble more than on a few occasions; the most memorable one of when he threw thumbtacks across the gymnasium floor, and a contagious grin that was permanently painted across his face no matter the emotion; even when he was angry and that was confusing to some, but not Shiloh, she knew her husband and loved him so fiercely she sometimes wondered if God would take him from her because she loved him too much.

Harbor drew her in again; this time Shiloh melted into his chest, her ear placed right over his heart to hear it's rhythmic beating. Harbor was a full foot taller and when he held her, she knew they were made for one another because of how seamlessly their bodies synced up; her head falling just at his heart and his chin resting atop her head. She could check his heart and he could protect her head; another way God had balanced them perfectly, for Shiloh was a bubbly free-spirited woman whose personality was entirely too big for her petite frame and her heart seemed to take up every inch of her small 5'0" stature. Even the dedicated brain space. She wasn't dumb by any means, her quick witty comebacks and problem-solving abilities were the very things that first attracted Harbor, well that is after the first thing; Shiloh's beauty.

Harbor was the definition of a hard worker. He had learned how to run heavy equipment at the ripe age of five and was driving a beat up '57 Chevrolet pickup whose gears caught more than the tires and seven year old Harbor would climb over into the engine bay and correct them before taking off again across the pasture land his family had owned for generations. Where his friends filled their summers with video games and frivolous play, Harbor filled his with hay baling and scrap metal collecting. Harbor had no interest in hobbies; *work* was his hobby.

When nineteen-year-old Harbor got Shiloh pregnant at seventeen and announced they were to be married, everyone wrote it off as quick as the Roadrunner could outrun Wiley Coyote. Yet here they stood, twelve years later inside a business they had bought and revived from the ashes, turning it into a fruitful venture.

The creaking of the metal door startled them, and they broke their hold of each other almost as quick as they found it.

"Boss Man, I can't get the air pressure to rise in number six." Wes, the sixty-three-year-old mechanic limped around from behind the door. Wes was as old as the trucks he worked on and as black as the grease that stained his uniform. He had dark wooly hair with tufts of white and a beard to match; his eyes similar to the color of the charred wood that lined the bottom of the burn barrel in the shop where he worked. Wes, along with the majority of the employees with the exception of two that Harbor had hired on, came under Harbor and Shiloh's commands when the business changed hands.

"Oh, 'scuse me," Wes chuckled as it donned on him that he had intruded on an intimate moment. Wes liked the married business pair, they were kind and generous, always loaning him money when he needed it and understanding when sickness plagued his body preventing him from work.

"Let's check it out." Harbor headed to the door and looking back laughed as Shiloh's cheeks filled with color.

"Shut up…" Shiloh smirked sheepishly shifting her weight to her left hip and crossing her arms. "Hey, wait! I can batch the first two trucks but you're gonna have to batch the rest. I've got to get the girls to school."

"UGH! Okay!" Harbor grunted as he stepped out of the door but missing the step he flew forward.

Harbor hit the bedroom floor with a loud thud again. How he wished it wasn't a dream. He wanted to either drift back to sleep and live there in the dream forever or never visit it again.

<h1 style="text-align:center">Nine</h1>

Jacob eased into the familiar parking spot he always occupied when stopping at Rick's Country Store to gather the necessities for a weekend at the cabin. This week had been trying with Delilah, constantly throwing herself at him and then mocking Jacob's manhood whenever he denied her. He wanted to prove himself to her; to shut her up once and for all, but he knew better, if he gave in, Delilah would be the last he proved himself to. She was too close to home and a few of the other loggers had eavesdropped on her attempts, in this small town, Jacob would surely be caught before sunrise. Frustrated and eager to get the weekend started, Jacob threw the truck into park and slammed the door behind him as he headed for the barred doors of the Country Store that sat just alongside highway 90.

"Hello." The attendant stood behind the counter working on slicing thin pieces of cheese off half of a wheel wrapped in red wax.

Jacob nodded without making eye contact and headed for the beer coolers that lined the back wall. The cool air hit his face and the smell of nitrous and cardboard filled his nostrils as he grabbed two cases of Bud Light. He walked to the front and set them on the counter and then started collecting the less important items on his mental checklist.

Jacob grabbed the same items as always; a pack of baby wipes, a gallon of water, a couple of cans of potted meat, and a sleeve of saltine crackers and headed back towards the counter to be rung up when a flash of blue caught his eye.

It was the wrapper of a Rice Krispy treat reflecting the sunlight from the doors.

I could gift the girl.

Jacob stood staring while he contemplated whether or not to show kindness to his captive when the attendant interrupted his internal debate.

"That's just awful." The attendant nodded towards the T.V. mounted to the wall beside the door.

Jacob looked at the screen and it appeared to be a news conference of some sort, a young man with three small children standing around him as he held another toddler in his arms. Jacob studied the attendant as he rang up his items and placed them in brown paper bags.

"You getting your plots ready for hunting season?" The attendant tried desperately at small talk.

"Yeah," Jacob grunted as he searched his wallet for the hundred he hid in the folds.

"$50.57"

Jacob tore the bill from his wallet and placed it in the attendant's outstretched hand and tucked the cases of beer under his arm as he grasped the remaining bags firmly in his hand. Jacob started for the door whenever the attendant reminded him of his change. Just then a familiar face flashed across the T.V. screen.

Shiloh's.

THAT LYING PIG!

Jacob scowled inwardly as he snatched the change from the attendant, causing coins to scatter across the concrete floor and the attendant telling him to keep that attitude at home next time.

Jacob ignored the old man hollering at him as he crossed the parking lot to his truck and threw Shiloh's things into the bed. Climbing into his truck he set his cases beside him and had already chugged one down before getting back on the highway. When he finally reached the cabin, he had finished six beers which had fueled his inner flame of malice too much to the point that it consumed him leading him to forget to put the truck in park before swinging his door open. The ground still in movement underfoot was the only reminder he had.

He slammed it into park and snatched the two cases from beside him. He made his way through the tall grass almost tripping on some briars before regaining his balance but causing him to spill some of his beer. Agitated when he finally reached the door, he kicked it in.

Shiloh had heard him coming down the drive. She heard his cussing and the slamming of brakes and doors. She began praying and continued to do so even after Jacob kicked the door off the hinges making her jump.

"You're a lying pig!" Jacob snarled as he sat the beer on the makeshift table.

Lord, please, help me to be slow to anger and to give soft answers.

Shiloh ended praying and looked at Jacob who stood bowed up, he resembled a dog ready to attack, the only thing missing was the foaming of his mouth.

"What did I lie about?" Shiloh asked smoothly.

"I asked you if you had any children." Jacob's fists were clenched so tight his knuckles had turned white.

Shiloh's heart dropped to the floor as her stomach rose to her throat. She felt heat rush to her face as she swallowed hard to keep from vomiting.

Lord, NO! Not my babies!

Jacob crossed the span between them in two long steps. Shiloh closed her eyes and braced herself to catch a jab to the side of her face yet flinched when she felt Jacob's fingers dig into her arms as he lifted her up and put his mouth next to her ear.

"And I thought about letting you go because you were different… But you're not. You're a lying pig just like the rest of them." His breathy words reeked the sweet stench of alcohol.

Shiloh snatched her head away from him and struggled to break free as panic took over, the more she struggled, the harder his nails dug into her skin until little rivers of blood trickled down.

஑௧

A knock on the door startled Harbor and provoked the dogs into a barking frenzy. Harbor had retired for the day, escaping his Sunday best and leaving nothing on but his boxers and a white undershirt.

"Just a minute," he hollered in the direction of the front door as he dug through baskets of clean clothes, not yet folded, for a pair of gym shorts. He heard Junior and Millie stampeding towards the door.

"Wait just a sec!" He stepped into his shorts as he made his way into the living room.

"Y'all don't ever open the door without me. You don't know who it is." He was tying the drawstrings whenever Junior made eye contact with him and snatched the door open. Junior and Millie stood at the door in only their underwear. Modesty hadn't developed in them yet.

An unfamiliar laughter erupted from the other side of the door causing Harbor to pick up the pace to reach it.

A tall woman stood at the top of the steps looking down at Millie, who wasted no time on polite manners, as she began inspecting the cookies inside the foiled plate she had brought. A bright white smile painted her soft pink lips as Junior bombarded her with questions and with each question, a soft answer followed.

Harbor cut off Junior's line of questions and he replied with an annoyed look.

"Can I help you?" Harbor shoed the children away.

"I'm Emily Sisters, we talked on the phone awhile back." She pushed her sunglasses atop her head as if they were a headband to hold back her blonde tresses.

"Oh, yeah. Nice to meet you." Harbor held out his hand to offer a shake.

She held up the platter full of cookies and raised her eyebrows while she smiled causing her green eyes to glisten.

"Oh, sorry 'bout that." He stepped out of the doorway, allowing her to pass.

He was unaware of the state of his house until his eyes swept over the floors that hadn't been vacuumed in... he couldn't remember. Clothes and shoes trailed from the front door to the bedrooms and blankets covered the couch and recliners from the "camp-in" the kids had the night before.

"Excuse the mess. Wasn't expecting company." He chuckled uncomfortably as he brushed his disheveled hair to the side with his fingers.

"That's okay! I grew up with four younger brothers and I'm the only woman in my fire station, so I know how hard it is to keep a house." She gave him a reassuring smile. Harbor laughed and began clearing the couch.

"I just wanted to bring these by and see if you needed any help with anything." She placed the platter on the coffee table littered with coloring sheets and dried Play-doh.

"Thanks."

"No problem."

ಬೂಲ

Jacob glared at Shiloh as she slept on the pallet formed from sheets he had taken from the different hotels he stayed at. Curiosity struck him, how could a person imprisoned sleep so soundly? He couldn't remember a time he had ever slept well. It seemed with each dusk as the black cover spread across the sky so did an eerie darkness in his mind. Nightmares plagued him and a constant nagging feeling of paranoia.

Shiloh was different than the Christians he grew up knowing. She was like Todd. Jacob thought of his first encounter with Todd. He had offered Jacob a water bottle his first day on the job. Jacob hadn't come prepared for the stifling heat or the non-stop hauling and didn't pack enough water bottles to make it through the rest of the day. His tongue cleaved to the roof of his mouth and his throat was dry as a peanut field in the middle of August in Alabama. Jacob didn't know how Todd could tell he was on the verge of a heat stroke, but he was sure glad he did.

Jacob had turned the water bottle up and in three long gulps the bottle collapsed. Todd later overheated and was forced into the position of manning the service truck. Jacob continued to study this odd man which carried himself in such stark contrast from the men surrounding them. Todd later would ask Jacob if he had a relationship with Christ and thus explaining the oddball.

Jacob remembered the day he himself became a Christian. He was eight. He recalled the stiff white robe that smelled of moth balls, the chlorine in the baptismal that filled the air of the back rooms tucked behind the stage. The feeling of butterflies fluttering in his stomach as he stood in line behind Mikey Simms and Becky Andrews breath on the collar of his neck as they packed into the tight stairwell of the baptismal.

He watched as Pastor Grimms took hold of Mikey's nose and Mikey's light brown curls turned to straight black noodles lying flat on his head.

The words spoken between them were muted as if Jacob was watching a movie with the volume turned off, only to be flipped back on full blast with the eruption of applause and "Amen" ringing out from the congregation seated in the wooden pews.

Pastor Grimms motioned for him next.

Jacob's stomach rose to his throat and he swallowed hard as he stepped into the baptismal. The warm welcome of the water calmed him as he neared the Pastor.

He looked out into the audience searching the faces until his gaze fell on the familiar wrinkly face of Maw sitting proudly in the second row and Pops occupying the corner of the pew and dozing off. Maw smiled wide and waved to Jacob while she nudged Pops. He grumbled but then followed suit by smiling and waving while sitting up straight in the pew.

Jacob looked into the Pastor's warm brown eyes and nodded at each question the Pastor asked just as he was coached to do.

What was the question?

Jacob barely caught a breath as he was dunked under the water. His eyes still open burned from the chlorine, causing him to panic. He didn't wait for the Pastor's assistance to come up. The congregation and the Pastor laughed when Jacob popped up out of the water spitting and sputtering and as he pushed through the water to the steps.

After drying off and somewhat shaking off the fear and embarrassment, Jacob thought about how he didn't feel any different. Maybe he hadn't stayed under long enough.

All of the children baptized were chauffeured into a small choir room and Pastor Grimms came in to speak with them. He stood, now dry and in casual dress, at the small hymnal stand at the front of the room. He attempted to comb over his wet and barely-there hair to conceal the baldness that spread from his bushy eyebrows to the crown of his head.

"You children are now children of God!" He held his hands up as if inviting them in for a hug. No one moved. "Congratulations and welcome to the family!" he chirped.

A small applause ignited with the three adults helping and spread to the children's hands.

Jacob glanced around; their faces seemed to glow. He wondered if he glowed.

"You are saved. Let no one try to tell you differently. Don't allow that doubt into your mind. Doubt is from the deceiver. Doubt is not of God."

The children nodded and Jacob followed suit.

He never had questioned it; until now. Shiloh spoke of God often and she prayed to Him even more. Jacob had never done that, or couldn't recall. Jesus was his fire escape. But to Shiloh, Jesus was friend.

Ten

Deputy's raspy bark woke Harbor and the full sun filtering in through the bedroom blinds caused a sense of panic. He reached for his phone which read 9:38, forcing him to pop out of bed. He staggered into the living room where the kids were still on the couch where they had fallen asleep the night prior while watching T.V.

"Y'all get up. We're gonna be late for church."

Satisfied with the stirring of Ann and Junior, he went to the kitchen to get some coffee. After spilling the grounds and cleaning up the mess he found that the children still hadn't woke.

"Ya'll! Get up!" he hollered.

All the children sat up sleepy eyes and Millie began to cry. He studied their faces which were all stained from last night's dinner.

"Did y'all not get baths like I told you?"

"Ugh… No, sir," Ann replied while rubbing the sleep from her eyes.

"Why not?!"

"Because there wasn't any water pressure and I came

to tell you, but you told me to get out cause you were on the phone.”

“Why didn't you come tell me when I got off the phone?”

Ann shrugged. “I guess I forgot.”

Harbor groaned as he went back into the kitchen to investigate the water pressure. He turned on the faucet and bursts of water caused the spout to shake until a small stream of water trickled out. Harbor cursed under his breath and he glanced at the time on the microwave; 9:43. He took a gulp of his coffee but realized all too late that time for cooling had not passed leaving him with a burnt pride and tongue.

“Dammit!” He sent the cup flying through the air into the sink splattering the countertops with coffee and shattering the silence.

“Ohh, you say a bat werd!” Junior stood wide-eyed in the dining room.

“Boy! Go get dressed!” Harbor steered Junior by his messy bed-head towards the living room where the girls were watching T.V.

“YA'LL! GET DRESSED NOOOOW!” Harbor yelled as he stared unbelieving at the children.

The children scattered.

Harbor entered his room in hopes of finding a pack of baby wipes from Millie's diaper days to clean their faces and skip baths.

Not too much later, on the way to church, the older girls bickering over the lyrics of a schoolyard rhyme and the younger two crying of hunger filled the eight passenger SUV. The constant noise made Harbor believe that one could combust from racket.

“That's enough! For the love of God, please shut your

mouths!" He peered at surprised faces through the rearview mirror.

"But Daddy, I hungry."

"I know, son. I'm trying to get to Jack's to get some breakfast."

The children were able to keep quiet for about a millisecond before they started up with something else. Luckily, Harbor had managed to slide into home base and place the orders before the children starved to death.

Harbor thanked the unhappy window cashier as he crept forward and out of the parking lot. He wondered how Shiloh had done it. She made it look so easy. He kept messing up.

"I wanted pancakes!" one of the children cried out. He couldn't tell which. They all sounded the same when they whined.

"You get what you get, and you don't pitch a fit."

Harbor slammed on brakes as the driver in front of him slammed theirs, barely bumping their bumpers but not soft enough to spare the drinks and breakfast from flying into the floorboard, dash, and Harbor.

At church, Harbor's slacks were soiled, which represented his attitude precisely. Unfortunately, Harbor's smart-mouthed cousin, Beau, didn't pick up on it as Harbor and the children made their way into the church doors.

"Harbor, man… did you even attempt to brush their hair?" Beau teased as he marveled at the disheveled appearances of the children who paid him no attention as they hurried to the nursery; all too eager to be away from their father.

Something snapped in Harbor. Beau's teasing was the final poke that pushed Harbor over the edge. Weeks of frustration and anger spilled out and Beau was the unlucky fool to catch it.

Harbor cut his eyes in Beau's direction, as fast as his eyes moved, his body followed. He grabbed Beau by his shoulders, driving him into the cream-colored wall. The impact from Beau's head caused a slight indention in the sheetrock and the sound of the men scuffling drew the congregation, already seated, into the hall. The elderly women gasped at the sight of the two men using one another as ramming tools and at the words spewing from Harbor's lips. The men of the church grabbed and snatched at the brawlers whose arms seemed as octopus tentacles, as soon as one was contained, another found its target, until they were able to disentangle the two.

Brother Jim took control of the situation, ordering all the congregation back to their pews. Beau was sent into the bathroom to get his tan suit back in order and to rinse his bruised face. Harbor was directed to the church office.

Harbor could hear the hum of familiar voices as he walked past the doors of the fellowship hall where the congregation sat, awaiting Sunday school. He took a seat in the olive green and mustard yellow high-back patterned chair that sat adjacent to Brother Jim's desk which was littered with books of a variety of topics.

Just like high school days.

He scoffed at the idea. He doubted his charming smile would work on the pastor.

Brother Jim entered the office and closed the door behind him. He ran his hand through his dark chestnut hair peppered with strands of silver. "What happened?" He pointed towards the hall with his thumb.

Harbor took a deep breath. Had he even breathed at all this morning? He sat up and rested his hands on his knees. He studied the rug at his feet. He recalled the day he and Shiloh had picked it out. She was wearing his favorite sundress that accentuated her petite frame. She had gone through the store touching each rug. He had picked at her asking why women had to touch everything?

"Because women make the world beautiful! If it were up to you, the world would be stiff and colorless," she poked back.

His world had become stiff and colorless without her. *God, I miss her.*

"Well?" Brother Jim called Harbor back into reality.

"He doesn't know when to shut up."

Brother Jim nodded as he walked past Harbor to his desk, stopping long enough to pull up his navy slacks as he took his seat in the leather swivel chair. He ran his hand through his hair again and tugged on his maroon and navy striped tie to loosen it then rested his hands on the arms of his chair as he leaned back.

"I know Beau's your cousin. I also know he can be annoying. But ya can't go off whooping and cussin' him. Especially in the church."

Harbor could hear the sincerity in his voice and something else, humor perhaps? Harbor had continued his deep breathing and with every inhale of stale church air, rationale accompanied it.

"Yeah, I know… I just… It's been hard trying to get a new routine. A sense of normalcy since…" Harbor couldn't bring himself to say it.

Brother Jim's brown eyes were no longer was fixed on Harbor but had fell to his own feet.

"We all miss her; she was a big part of our church," Brother Jim said softly.

A flash of anger drove Harbor out of his chair and

onto his feet. He stood up looking down at Brother Jim.

"Y'all have NO idea! You only notice her absence whenever you don't have a teacher for the kids Sunday school or whenever y'all see me and the kids. I'm tired of everyone treating us differently and I'm sick of the feeling of everyone walking on eggshells!"

Brother Jim stood now and held his hands up as if he offered an apologetic sacrifice. "Harbor, I didn't mean…"

"No, of course you didn't. But I'm telling you. None of this makes sense. Ain't none of this right!" Harbor jabbed his finger towards Brother Jim as tears puddled in his eyes.

"Harbor, please," Brother Jim called after him as Harbor left the office blinking back tears.

Harbor made it to the nursery, much to the children's surprise.

"Y'all come on," Harbor demanded in a tone that kept the nursery worker silent to questions. But not Junior.

"Church is already over?!" he marveled as Ann gathered up Millie and Nora collected their discarded shoes.

"No, we're leaving," he snapped, quieting anymore questions.

꽈

"How can you be so calm? Don't you know what I can do to you? How easily I could end your life and go about mine as if nothing happened?"

"Could you?" Shiloh raised her eyebrows as she focused on opening her pack of crackers.

Jacob stared as the satisfaction of proving it to her dangled in front of him as a bloody steak to a starving dog.

But something prevented him, keeping his abusive hands tethered. As soon as he could figure it out, he'd allow himself the satisfaction.

He charged Shiloh but she didn't flinch. He snatched her up and she inhaled sharply as he dug his fingernails into her arms before setting her back down.

"Don't forget it," he sneered.

She gave him a pitiful look. "If you were going to kill me, you would've already done it. You wanna know why you haven't been able to?"

Jacob stared at her in disbelief.

She placed another Vienna sausage atop a cracker. "Because God hasn't allowed you to."

Jacob scoffed. "Where was your God that day at the lake? Or when parents die in wrecks? Or when children are diagnosed with cancer?"

Jacob uncrossed his arms to pull another beer out of the cardboard box.

She finished chewing her food before swallowing a gulp of water.

"That's a good question. One I've asked often as I've stared at these four walls. One I used as an excuse as I plotted your murder and my escape."

He sat up at the mention of his murder.

She continued, "That's a question I had never really thought of the answer, until now. When others asked me, I would quote scripture and tell them, *Oh, you just gotta trust it's all gonna work out for your good…* A parent burying their baby doesn't want to hear that. A child being bounced from foster home to foster home can't hang onto that when they're scared and alone in a house full of strangers. Me, I can't understand how my being raped is going to be for my good. But I do know this. Nowhere in the Bible does it say we will be without persecution or hard times. Actually, it says the opposite. It seems to convey the idea that the Christian life is full of hard times. So, my answer to your question, one I've been struggling with myself, comes down to this: God protects me from nothing, but sustains me in everything."

Eleven

I wish it were easier, Harbor thought to himself as he searched for the credit card scanner to hook up to his phone. An impatient customer stood on the other side of the desk waiting to pay for his gravel. Harbor swore he could feel his breath on the back of his neck, regardless of him standing in front of him.

"I'm sorry. My wife usually does this." Harbor dug around in Shiloh's desk drawer.

God, how can one person be so unorganized?!

Harbor grit his teeth as he pulled out an emery board and a nearly empty pack of bobby pins.

"Whatcha hunting?" Emily emerged from the back office with a box full of files and outdated maintenance booklets headed to the dump. Harbor was pleased with the work she had completed in the batch house. She organized it so neat that when she finished, he asked her to move onto the office. There was one exception, Shiloh's desk. He now learned that he regretted that decision.

"I'm trying to find the dang card reader. Shi never kept anything in the same place."

Emily set the box down on the corner of the desk and

came around to help find the reader amongst the drawer full of receipts, empty pens, paperclips, and junk.

He could feel the heat rising in his cheeks as he stood close enough to her that he could smell the sweet fragrance her gold tresses put off.

Her hand brushed against his by accident, or was it? He hadn't flirted in so long he had forgotten how to pick up on clues or body language.

He pulled his hand out of the drawer when an image of Shiloh flashed in his mind.

"Found it!" Emily pulled the reader out from the back of the drawer, holding it up as if she held a championship trophy.

"Thanks," Harbor replied when she dropped it into his outstretched hand.

After he finished up with the customer, he found Emily in the back office organizing a shelf. He stood in the doorway admiring her beauty and work; he thought how awkward it would be if he got caught staring. He'd be classified as a creeper for sure.

Clearing his throat, she swung her gaze over her shoulder.

"Hey! Can you hand me that?" She nodded in the direction of a parts manual as she held the others on the shelf in place.

"Yeah…" Harbor picked up the thick book using more strength than he had anticipated. "Here, lemme get it." He slid it into place as a whiff of her scent trailed into his nose again, sending his mind swimming.

"Thanks. You showed up just in time." She smiled at her work as she wiped the dust from her hands.

"Whatcha think?" She nodded towards the organized shelf.

"Looks real good." Butterflies and a wave of nausea filled his stomach as he searched the wall for the words. "Hey, Em?" He kept his eyes fixed on the bookshelf.

"Yeah?"

"Would you like to get dinner?" The words fumbled out of his mouth quicker than he could process them.

What would people say? It'd only been three months since Shi's disappearance. But he had needs. He had children who had needs. Before he could retract his question, she interrupted his mental wrestling match.

"Sure."

"Okay. Meet you at the BBQ place on Chestnut at six thirty?"

She paused.

He regretted asking. What kind of man did she think he was now?

"Or… I could cook for you and the kids?"

Harbor shifted his body to face her. He hadn't noticed her height until standing right next to her, she was almost as tall as him. He looked into her sea green eyes.

"That'd be nice. It's been awhile since we've had a good, home cooked meal… at our own home."

She laughed. "You can't cook?"

He held up his calloused, greasy hands. "What do you think?"

They laughed and he tried to remember the last time he had laughed like this. He thought when Shiloh disappeared so would his desires for laughter, life, and love. Yet here he was; living and laughing. Could it be possible that he love again?

Later that morning, Harbor jumped at the ringing of his phone. The caller I.D. read "Det. Harris." Harbor slid the bubble on his phone to answer.

"Hello."

"Mr. Romans."

"Yeah."

"Hey, I was just calling to touch base."

"Yeah?" Harbor set the wrench down on the tool bench and listened intently.

"Well, we haven't got any new leads but we're still working on finding your wife."

"Yeah… thanks." He picked the crowbar up.

"Yes, sir. Mr. Romans-"

Click.

Harbor hung up the phone, fastening it to the clip that hung from his side. He went back to work replacing the shredded mess of a tire on his mixer truck.

"This summa heat sho is doing a numba on our tires," Wes said as he handed Harbor the air wrench.

"Yeah, we're gonna have to start pouring earlier before the asphalt heats up too much."

The blazing August Alabama sun seemed to place a heat seal on what Harris had avoided saying, but what Harbor had accepted; Shiloh was not coming back. Harbor let the mechanical whir of the wrench fill the space void of conversation between him and his mechanic.

"Boss?"

"Huh?"

"You done hit them all."

Harbor examined the lug nuts on the tire.

"Yeah. Looks good."

"Yous alright?"

"Yeah, Im gonna be." Harbor handed the wrench back to him as he turned to walk away.

"My ol' lady and I been praying for you. I can see somedays when you need it more than others." Wes's last attempt of getting his young boss to open up.

Harbor swung his head over his shoulder. "Thanks, make sure that tire has plenty of air in it."

Harbor put the kids to bed after they enjoyed the home cooked meal prepared by Emily. Making his way back to the kitchen he had forgotten for a brief moment that Shiloh wasn't the one he would find cleaning and putting away dishes. The sight of Emily easily reaching the top shelf of the mahogany stained cabinets jerked him back into reality. His back tightened and his shoulders broadened as the thought of Shiloh never coming back crossed his mind.

He shook his head and pushed himself to the sink beside her.

"Thanks for the supper. It was really nice."

"Ah, it was nothing. I enjoyed it. Your children are as precious as Shiloh described them." She kept her focus on the plate she was drying.

Harbor stepped closer. "Yeah, they're something else."

He was close enough to feel the heat coming from her body which was perfumed with lovely floral notes.

She placed the plate in the cabinet and turned around, resting her palms and butt on the edge of the countertop.

"You're really blessed." She studied the pictures on the walls where framed snapshots of birthday celebrations and family barbecues hung. Allowing her to the luxury of snippets of their lives before tragedy struck.

Harbor turned around to see what she saw, but he saw more. He remembered how he and Shiloh had stayed up late the previous night putting together Ann's first bicycle. He recalled how Shiloh wanted to put it together freehanded, but he insisted on her reading the manual. He remembered when he was pulling the last of the chicken off the grill at the July Fourth barbecue and Nino jumped from Shiloh's lap onto the table. In his attempt to snag the chicken thigh from the pan in Harbor's hand, knocked it to the ground. He recalled how Shiloh kissed him repeatedly to make him turn his frustrated frown into a smile and to prevent him from killing her gluttonous pug.

"Yeah. I was." He didn't want to think or talk about Shiloh. It made his chest tight and his eyes sting.

"I'm sorry. I didn't mean to…" Emily's gaze fell to her feet.

He stood in front of her and gently took her by the chin, locking his eyes with hers.

"Hey, it's okay. It's getting better."

Offering a crooked grin, he swallowed hard at the color that flushed her cheeks. Her breath became shallow and his heartbeat pounded so loud he was sure she could hear it. Pulling her chin towards him, her body followed and he leaned forward.

"Daddy, I firsty." Junior had one more demand for the night.

Emily jerked back and Harbor spun around.

"Uh, yeah. Come here and get it." He grabbed a cup from the cupboard.

"Drink it up and back to bed. No more getting up tonight."

Junior nodded as he finished his water and waddled back to bed.

"I'm gonna go," she whispered, and she began to gather her things.

"No, you're fine." He reached for her hand.

She let him hold it for a moment.

"Harbor…" a sympathetic smile spread. "You are feeling a lot of stuff right now. I don't think you want to do this. Heck, I'm not sure I want to do this."

"I'm pretty sure I know what I want to do," he laughed. He tried to pull her into his embrace but she resisted.

"No. You need to halt."

"What?"

"I've got a friend who sees a therapist and her advice to him was, when you are hungry, angry or anxious, lonely, or tired, you halt."

He stared at her expressionless.

"Harbor, you're lonely and tired. It's been three months since Shiloh disappeared and you've been doing it all by yourself ever since. You don't want me, and to be honest, I don't want you. No offense. But until we know for a fact what's happened to Shiloh, I don't want to run the risk of her coming back and I lose two friends."

He thought for a moment before responding and dropped her hand.

"Yeah. I agree… Well, let me walk you to the door."

A faint smile broke out and she kissed his cheek. He watched her from the door until her taillights disappeared. He was alone, again.

Twelve

Jacob leaned against the wall as he perched atop the edge of the table. One leg pulled up with his foot steadying him from help by the 2x4 table leg with his other foot planted firmly on the floor balancing him.

"You don't know my past," he snapped as he looked through Shiloh, avoiding eye contact.

"Then why don't you tell me?"

"Why should I?" he scoffed.

"Why don't you? Who am I gonna tell?" She pulled on the chain wrapped around her leg.

Jacob thought for a moment as his chest began tightening.

"Come on. For real, we both know I'm not going to make it out of here alive. You might as well tell me."

"You're right. So why bother?" he snapped.

He needed something. The tightening in his chest was causing him to become short of breath and he wouldn't be able to argue much longer. But still, something had his feet chained to the floor, unable to escape; just as he had Shiloh.

Shiloh answered slowly, as if she herself had pondered her persistence for the first time. "I guess to maybe be of some help?" She shrugged.

He rolled his eyes and chuckled. "You've been so helpful." He glanced her over.

Shiloh didn't flinch.

A wave of heat crossed Jacob's face at Shiloh's coolness. What was with this girl? She had no fear. Jacob regretted the comment.

"So?" She sat as a child awaiting story time at the local library Maw used to take Jacob to. All her attention focused on him and what he had to say.

Jacob feared his chest would explode from the pressure pushing from inside. He likened himself to a kettle with boiling water and he needed to depressurize. Before he could remove himself from the heat, preventing blowing a loud whistle, his lips betrayed him and his past began spewing out; out of his control and he revisited a place he swore he'd never go again.

"Jacob," his mother bit at him, "get in here now!"

Jacob hurried from the kitchen, abandoning the condiments and sandwich meat laid out on the counter where he had begun to prepare supper for the two of them.

Jacob's mother leaned against the doorway to the living room as she took a drag off her Virginia Slim cigarette. Her cut-off blue jean shorts seemed to stop where her long legs began and the dingy white tank top fit snug over her braless torso.

"What's wrong?" Jacob asked looking past her teased blonde hair, observing that her black roots were showing before fixing his attention to her stoic face.

"Me and the girls are going out tonight, the Elks Lodge is having a ladies night, drinks are half off." She took another drag of her cigarette, exaggerating the wrinkles that seemed to point directly to their cause.

"Mara, you got a light?" Jill was Mara's friend since middle school and was always in close proximity, circling the area like a buzzard waiting to pick off any discarded dead thing.

Mara tossed her lighter onto the cushion beside Jill who sat comfortably on the outdated patterned couch.

"Okay…" Jacob searched her face for a hidden message and when Mara grew impatient with his incompetence.

"You have to drive us." Her head bobbed with each word.

Jacob's jaw twitched.

He had planned on eating his sandwich and retiring to the solitude of his bedroom away from Jill's beady eyes and Mara's constant demands. He had no desire to chauffeur drunk women around or to be pawed at by strange middle-aged women.

"Ma, I can't," Jacob attempted to argue.

Mara shifted all her weight onto her left foot and fixed her hand on her hip, leaning forward she hissed, "Excuse me?"

"Ma, I'm only fifteen and I don't have a learner's permit," he replied.

Mara stood straight and rested one hand on Jacob's shoulder, "If you can drive yourself to the gas station to get snacks, you can drive us to the lodge," she chided.

"The store ain't but a half mile down a country back road. The lodge is on the other side of town on the highway. If we get pulled over, I won't never get my license."

"I suggest you don't do anything to get us pulled over then."

Jill cracked a laugh that reminded Jacob of the caw of a buzzard.

Mara left the conversation and the doorway to cross the room and put out her cigarette. She turned to see Jacob still standing where she had left him.

"Why are you still standing there? Go get ready."

Jacob clenched his jaw and fists. He felt his blood boiling and his anger bubbling, on the verge of eruption.

Mara picked up on it. "Jacob."

Jacob imagined that was how his mother would have woken him up from his nap as a toddler, lulling his name while caressing his back. He didn't know though. He had lived with his grandparents since birth. Mara was only thirteen when she had him and moved out to live with her boyfriend shortly after she turned fourteen, leaving Jacob behind for her parents to raise.

Pop was a hardworking man who drank too much and liked to play his three-stringed guitar all hours of the night. Three strings because over time he had broken every other one strumming it too hard and Maw wouldn't give him the money to replace them in hopes that he would break the rest and forget his drunken solo performances.

Maw was kind to Jacob but peculiar about what he did and who he played with. Jacob pondered if she was over-protective of him because how Mara turned out. Jacob remembered Pop taking him to the general store one year for his birthday and letting him pick something out. Jacob had chosen a toy cap gun, delighted each time he pulled the trigger to hear a loud pop and the smell of sulfur filling the air. When Maw arrived home from the women's luncheon and saw the gun, horrified she took it and handed Jacob a boy baby doll. Pop's shoulders slumped in defeat as he walked away. Jacob knew that would be the last he ever saw of the toy gun; Maw ran the house and could nag something fierce.

Both were killed in a car accident last summer resulting in Jacob's new normal. *Mara.*

"Please. Go. Get. Ready." A feigned sympathetic look on her face.

Jacob rolled his eyes in aggravation and struck the door frame as he turned to walk away. The eruption of anger and the loud thump made Mara jump and Jill caw.

Loud twangy music blared and the clamor of glasses clinking and women laughing spilled out the doors of the brick building with Elks Lodge 66 in faded red letters. Mara and Jill murmured and cackled, quickly making their way up the cracked concrete walkway to the doors. Jacob made his way up the walkway observing the grass that managed to grow in the cracks. The mixture of cigarettes and cheap perfumes turned his stomach and he wondered if he could go home and just come back in a couple of hours to pick them up.

He stopped, looking at the light pole, he saw a swarm of bugs hovering around its glow.

"Jacob. Come on, I want you to meet my friends." Mara stood in the door waving him in, she already had a drink in hand.

Jacob let out a sigh and made his way in.

The dim room helped frame the lit stage where a live band performed. Three middle-aged men wearing ten-gallon cowboy hats resembling thumbtacks swayed back and forth, tapping their feet while singing and playing guitars, the drummer nodded his head every once in a while. Women, in an obvious attempt to seem younger, wore tight blue jeans and low-cut shirts revealing wrinkled cleavage. Mara and Jill were the younger women and easily drew the attention of the male patrons, Mara more so than Jill.

"This is my boy!" Mara squealed at the group of ladies gathered at the bar. They all fixed their eyes on Jacob. Jacob felt awkward as the women commented on his appearance.

"Oh, Mara! He's so handsome! Is he eighteen yet?" The woman who asked looked to be in her mid-forties.

"He looks like he could be your boyfriend!" Another exclaimed. Mara took it as a compliment to her youthful appearance and not at her son's mature looks.

"How old are you boy?" a heavyset woman leaning against the bar with a beer bottle in hand inquired.

"Fifteen," Mara chirped.

"Jailbait!" the first woman cracked.

A group of men came through the door about that time and stole the attention away from Jacob, he was grateful to become invisible again.

While scanning the room for the sign that pointed to the bathroom his eyes met with Jill's, she was staring at him with her beady eyes again but this time with her lips curled, an uneasy feeling washed over Jacob and he felt the color drain from his face but acted as if he didn't see her watching him. He found the sign for the bathroom and hastily made his way to it, safe from uncomfortable gazes.

The one stall, one urinal bathroom reeked of urine. While Jacob washed his hands, he studied the face staring back curiously at him from the streaky mirror to see what the women at the bar were enticed by. Jacob had never given much thought to his appearance but as he studied his reflection, he realized he did look like a college-aged man. His dark wavy hair connected to his five o'clock shadow and his grey eyes were outlined by thick eyelashes. A strong jaw sat atop his thick neck which spilled into broad shoulders. He had aged dramatically after the death of his grandparents.

The door almost hitting him snatched him from his thoughts.

"Whoa. Sorry bud." One of the thumbtacks entered and fixed himself in front of the urinal.

"No problem," Jacob replied as he caught the door and step into the drunken masses.

Jacob passed the hours and avoided Jill's eyes by taking a seat behind a blown speaker and played on his phone. Just as his phone's battery died the band ended their song and the bartender announced the bar would be closing shortly and that all tabs needed to be paid. Jacob came out of his hiding place and scanned the room for Mara when he felt a hand slide up the inside of his arm. He turned his head to find Jill looking up at him. He pulled away.

"Where's Ma?"

Jill nodded towards the door where Mara was tangled up with one of the guitar-playing thumbtacks, they broke it up long enough to make it out the door.

"You've got to take me home," Jill slurred.

Jacob felt heat rising into his cheeks. He balled his fists and stared towards the door.

"Fine. Come on," he hissed through clenched teeth.

Jill staggered behind Jacob to the car, slurring country songs loudly. She slumped into the passenger seat and seemed to have fallen asleep by the time they reached the highway a quarter mile away.

Good. Now she'll shut up. I'm not getting her out. She can sleep in here, Jacob thought. But when he pulled into the driveway, Jill popped up.

Jacob didn't acknowledge her and put the car in park, got out, and closed the driver's door. Jill settled back into the seat. Exhausted he made his way through the narrow-paneled hall to his bedroom, undressing to his boxers when he reached his bedside and falling into his bed, he quickly fell to sleep.

Startled, he was awakened by the weight of someone straddling him. He heard a familiar laugh, it sounded as a buzzard cawing. Adrenaline filled his veins and his skin prickled; he pulled his arms from his sides only to have them snatched back down. He bucked like the broncos at the local rodeo Pop used to take him to every summer, but to no avail. Jill had tied him to the metal bed frame.

Sadness, shame, and anger paralyzed Jacob as he laid still, his shaking chest and a single tear that ran from the corner of his eye, past his temple and absorbed into his chocolate waves, was the only proof he was still alive. Jill slipped back into her floral-patterned blouse and shimmied into her jeans.

"You're okay. You're a man now. You're welcome," she whispered as she loosened the robe sash and belt from around Jacob's wrists.

Jacob stared at the ceiling. "I didn't want to." His voice cracked.

"You sure about that?" Jill chuckled. "Your mind may not have wanted to, but your body said otherwise. I just helped you along." She stood at the foot of his bed with her arms crossed.

Confusion clouded Jacob's mind. He hated Jill, but his

body had betrayed him.

"No." Jacob shook his head from side to side. He sat up and snatched the quilt that Maw had made him years ago that laid at the foot of his bed. Covering himself up, "Get out," he snapped.

"Whatever. Quit acting like a baby." She rolled her eyes as she went out the door and slammed it behind her.

Jacob sat on the side of his bed in the darkness for hours as waves of emotion crashed into him. Wading through them until a wave of anger drowned him. He pushed himself off his bed and scooped his clothes up. After he dressed, he pried his bedroom door open slowly and crept down the hall. Peering into the living room he saw Jill's sleeping outline on the couch. Stepping lightly towards her he bumped into the coffee table rattling the glass ashtray that sat atop it. Jill rolled over, now facing Jacob.

He held his breath.

Jill settled into the couch and her shallow breathing resumed.

Jacob took another step forward.

"What are you doing?" Mara had slipped in quietly through the backdoor and was now standing in the hall looking into the living room where Jacob was bent over Jill asleep on the couch.

Jacob straightened and the accusation fell from his lips faster than his mind could process it.

"Jill made me have sex with her." Jacob searched Mara's face for sympathy, anger, something from his mother.

Jill, awake now, sat up with a look of shock painted across her face and then she began to stream crocodile tears, "How could you say such a thing?!" she gasped.

Jacob's gaze of disbelief bounced back and forth from Jill to Mara.

Mara didn't even look at Jill, her eyes fixed on Jacob.

"You're a liar! Jill is like an aunt to you! YOU. YOU'RE THE ONE I CAUGHT STANDING OVER HER LIKE SOME CREEPER!" Mara had made her way to Jacob and was now screaming and poking her finger at him.

Jacob pushed her away and she stumbled before regaining her balance.

"GET OUT! I WON'T LIVE IN THE SAME HOUSE WITH A PERVERT!"

Tears welled in Jacob's eyes and he ran out the front door.

Thirteen

"Aunt Rena is here!" Harbor hollered as he took a pack of frozen chicken thighs out of the deep freezer. "Ya'll hurry up!" He laid the thighs in the sink.

"Chicken, AGAIN?" Junior came into the kitchen tugging on his monster truck shirt.

"You can just not eat," Harbor scoffed.

"I tired of chicken," Junior pleaded as he rummaged around in the dishwasher for his favorite cup.

"Well, that's what we got." Harbor pulled the milk jug out of the fridge and Junior handed him his orange cup.

Rena made her way through the house collecting discarded clothes and forgotten dishes, putting them into the laundry hampers and beside the sink already overflowing with dirty dishes. Harbor nodded thankfully at her. Shiloh's aunt was more like a mother to Shiloh and a grandmother to Harbor and Shiloh's children.

"Girls! Ya'll come on now," Harbor groaned.

"Yes, sir, we're coming. We're coming," Ann called from her bedroom as her and Nora came out with arms full of laundry heading for the washroom.

"Ain't no way all them are dirty." Harbor flattened himself to the wall as they passed by him in the hall. The girls didn't respond as they tiptoed, careful not to trip up on the toys and dog underfoot. The sound of a plastic cup and its contents hitting the floor stopped Harbor in his tracks.

"Uh-oh. I spilt it," Junior called out.

Harbor felt the heat rising from his toes as he fought blowing his top in front of sweet Rena.

"Clean. It. Up," he said through clenched teeth.

Why is EVERY morning chaos?

Rena met Harbor at Millie's bedroom door cradling Millie in her arms, a worrisome look painted Rena's face.

"What's wrong?" Harbor studied Millie's sleepy face.

Rena lipped, "She feels feverish."

Harbor gently cupped Millie's forehead, she flinched from his icy touch and the heat radiating from her tiny head warmed Harbor's hand that was still cold from the frozen chicken.

"You not feeling good, baby?" Harbor asked Millie softly.

Millie shook her head and turned into Rena's body.

Harbor thought for a moment.

I've got a full schedule today. Ain't no way I can take her to the doctor.

Rena was studying Millie and stroking her hair, so Harbor waved to call her to attention, she acknowledged him.

"You watch her and give her some Tylenol?" Harbor asked while stumbling through some of the sign language letters he had learned.

Rena smiled and nodded. Grateful that Harbor had tried to communicate with her.

Harbor signed a quick, "thank you." and answered his phone that had been ringing.

Chaos still ensued in the background and in order to not seem unprofessional and to hear the caller on the other end more clearly, Harbor made his way outside. The summer sun was blinding and Harbor squinted as he made his way across the yard.

"Romans Ready Mix."

"Harbor?"

"Speaking."

"You ain't gonna believe this man. I was going thro-"

Harbor cut him off, the caller was speaking so fast and excitedly Harbor couldn't recognize his voice.

"Who is this?"

"Clay." One of the fish suppliers of the lake, Harbor had sold him some gravel a time or two and they always chatted when Harbor ran into him at the bait store. "Harbor you ain't gonna believe it, man!"

"What?" Harbor chuckled at his excitement. Harbor figured he was about to be on the receiving end of a fisherman's tale that would surpass all the lies he had heard over the years at the bait store.

"You know that Blann sometimes lets me hunt out there since I help him out with keeping the lake stocked."

"Yeah?" This was new information to Harbor. He didn't know anyone hunted out there.

"Well, I went out there yesterday evening to collect my game cameras and I was going through the images this morning and I've got him! I've got him on camera!"

"Oh, yeah? How many points?" Harbor kicked at the chickens as he started towards the office to retrieve their feed.

"What? No. Not a buck, Harbor. The guy who took Shiloh!"

Harbor froze. Time froze.

Harbor's ears began ringing and his pulse quickened. His heart rose to his throat and he tried to swallow it back down. He tried clearing his throat, but all his efforts were thwarted by the thick humidity in the air. He sat down on the office concrete steps, warm from the sun.

"You hear me? You there?" Harbor could hear Clay's smile.

Finally, after what seemed to be an eternity.

"Y-Yea. I-I hear ya. Are you sure?" Harbor stumbled over the words.

The world surrounding Harbor seemed to intensify. The bug's buzz, the bird's chirping, the leaves rustling, the mixer trucks firing up, even the sun seemed too loud. Harbor wanted to scream for everything to stop. He tried to hone in on what Clay was saying.

"Yeah, man. The dates and time ain't wrong in it! You wanna come over and look at them? I've got his truck I know for sure! I haven't finished going through them, but I know it, man!"

Harbor fought through the fog of questions that clouded his mind.

Is she alive? Do I know this guy? How do I find her? How do I find him? No, it can't be right.

"What do you see in them?" Harbor didn't want to run after a false hope. "Why are you just now bringing this up? Did Harris not ask you for these?" Harbor asked sharply. Clay wasn't cut, his excitement mimicking a shield to which none could cut through. Harbor could hear the clicking of the mouse as Clay made his way through the game camera images. Clay spoke slowly.

"I see Shiloh."

Harbor blinked the tears back.

"I see a blue Dodge Ram."

Harbor tried to think of anyone he knew that might have a truck matching that description.

"I see a man with a tree limb in his hand."

Harbor closed his eyes tight.

"I see… I think we need to call Harris."

Harbor opened his eyes to see Rena with Millie in tow and the other kids coming out of the house next-door.

"Yeah. I'll do that now. Bring all of it over here now!" Harbor replied as he hung up the phone.

"Bye, Daddy!" Each of them attempting to cry louder than the other.

Harbor contemplated telling Rena what he had just learned.

"Bye, ya'll. Behave. I'll be by to pick you up after while." Harbor stood while looking in his phone's contacts for Harris' number. He found it and dialed.

Clay pulled in followed by Harris' Tahoe. Harbor hadn't moved from the steps of the office. He watched as Clay gathered up memory cards from his passenger seat and made his way up the walk.

"You alright?" Clay asked sheepishly.

Harbor wanted to pummel him.

Why hadn't he thought of the game cameras before?! What if Shiloh is dead and it's because they waited too long! But Harbor only nodded and kept his eyes fixed on the Tahoe as Harris opened the door and stepped out, holding a legal pad and a laptop.

"How's it going?" Harris asked as he walked up. "Where can we sit down and look at these?"

Harbor nodded towards the office and led the way up the steps with Clay and Harris close behind.

"You can sit here." Harbor motioned towards Shiloh's desk; he hadn't touched anything since her disappearance. Harris sat and set up the laptop while Clay laid the memory cards beside the laptop and Harbor took a seat at his desk that sat across the room from Shiloh's.

Harbor observed how out of place Harris looked behind Shiloh's desk. Shiloh had all of her office necessities within arm's reach and because Harris seemed three times the size of Shiloh, he knocked things over with his elbows. Harbor chuckled as he thought Harris resembled Alice whenever she ate the carrot making her grow out of the windows in Wonderland.

After setting things right that he made amiss, Harris opened his black laptop and typed something before selecting one of the memory cards and inserting it into the side of his laptop. Harbor kept his seat at his desk but could see the images from the reflection in the mirror behind Harris.

Harbor's pulse beat loudly as the pictures flashed in the mirrors, drowning out Harris' voice. He wondered if the two men filling up the tight quarters could hear it. He closed his eyes tightly as the reflection of when Shiloh was struck by the stranger appeared.

She didn't see it coming… She couldn't even put up a fight. *Oh, Shi. Oh, God.*

"Harbor, you hear me?" Harris asked

Harbor opened his eyes to Harris and Clay's concerned expressions.

"Huh?"

"I said; We got him. Somebody's gonna be able to identify him."

"I hope you're right."

"I'm going to take these back to the station and start

running a search for offenders with this kinda truck."

Clay nodded and looked towards Harbor who nodded in agreement.

"It's important that we keep this quiet though, okay?"

"Why? Shouldn't we be asking folks if they know anybody with that truck? Cover more ground, ya know?" Clay piped up and looked back and forth between Harbor and Harris.

"No."

"NO?!" Harbor snorted.

"How do you catch a dog? Do you make a bunch of noise or do you quietly slide the noose around its neck?" Harris raised an eyebrow.

"Gotcha." Clay agreed and Harbor nodded.

"Trust me. We're gonna find him. We're gonna find your wife."

<h1 style="text-align:center">Fourteen</h1>

Harris entered the station with only the rapping of his heels on the tiled floor and the smell of coffee brewing to greet him. He quickly made his way down the long corridor to the elevator. He sighed under his breath, "Could've taken the stairs and it would've been faster."

He fidgeted with the memory cards in his pocket as he watched the numbers on the panel light up until a ding rang out and the doors opened in front of him.

"Mornin' Harris!" Kim chirped.

"Mornin.'" Harris passed by her unwilling for small talk.

"You're in a hurry this morning," she teased as she stepped passed him into the elevator fluffing her white hair in the mirrored walls.

"Yes, ma'am. I'm sorry." Harris swung behind his shoulder offering an apologetic smile. He liked Mrs. Kim, she was the station momma and dispatch. He didn't mean to seem rude. She gave an understanding nod and a wave while the doors closed.

Harris fumbled with his keys until he found the one that unlocked his office door. He sat his briefcase on his desk as he slid the computer out. In his haste he had forgotten about the paper cup still half full with cold coffee from last night's late hours, spilling it across his desk.

He bit his lip to keep from cussing and worked frantically to contain the black liquid spreading on his papers leaving them with an antique finish.

After cleaning the mess as best he could with the leftover fast food napkins he found stuffed in his desk, he sat down and opened his computer. He slid a memory card in and studied the pictures of the truck closely. He dialed the DMV downstairs and requested a list of owners who had registered a blue Dodge Ram year models 2000-2005.

"Oh, Harris… this list is never ending. You want me to print it?" the friendly clerk asked.

Thoughts pinged around Harris's mind until he got a hole-in-one.

"No. That's alright. I don't have time to scan it. Thanks, though." He hung up the receiver only to pick it back up and dial again.

Harris pulled into the gravel parking lot and parked his truck next to Blann's pickup. Making his way to the front of the building, Blann met him at the door.

"Hey, man. Come on in." Blann led the way to his office and motioned for Harris to the seat in the chair in front of his desk.

"Blann, I've got some pictures here and if you see anything familiar, just let me know."

Harris began to pull the pictures from the manilla folder whenever a rap on the door interrupted him.

"Blann, the skidder went down and the guys wanna know if you want to shut 'er down for the day?"

Blann nodded and waved his wife away. "Close the

door!" he hollered after her when she left it ajar.

Harris slid the pictures across the desk and Blann leaned over them. His eyebrows rose and he pushed a hard blow through his lips before sitting back and staring at Harris.

"What?"

"I know that truck."

"Yeah?"

"And I know the guy. It's one of my former workers. Jacob Solomon."

"Do we have any idea where we might can find this guy?" Deputy Strickland asked as he drummed his pen on the table in front of him.

"We know he has used his card pretty regularly at Roger's Country Store on the corner of 45 and 80. I figur-"

The door to the conference room slung open and Ms. Kim stepped in out of breath. Harris focused on her as beads of sweat on her forehead proved that the news she had couldn't wait for the ancient elevator resulting in her climbing three flights of stairs to the conference room.

"I just got a call from a young man that said him and his girlfriend…" She took a deep breath before continuing, "Were out on county road 29 right past mile marker 114 when an older white guy in a pickup truck matching the description of the BOLO ran them off from an overgrown drive."

"How long ago?"

She wiped her forehead. "That's the thing. About three months ago!"

"29?" Harris turned to the oversized map plastered on

the wall behind him. He traced the map's roads with his finger until he found county road 29. "29 is a cut through about twenty miles down 45!" He chugged the rest of the lukewarm coffee that sat on the pedestal in front of him. "Load up boys. We got 'em."

ဆ)ભ

Shiloh's eyes stung from emotional tears caused by Jacob's recollection of his childhood. No wonder he went crazy. Sympathy, anger, and something else, perhaps understanding, took turns motivating her words she spoke.

"I'm so sorry that happened to you." She shook her head and tried to keep her voice from cracking.

Jacob perched on the corner of the makeshift table, his face emotionless. As if he had read someone else's story instead of shining a light on some personal shadows.

She studied him. What did he need from her? What could she say? She thought of her own abuse and the healing that came from seeing a therapist. She remembered the success she had with EMDR therapy but disregarded it. He would never go along with it. She recalled what helped her to even begin to open up to her therapist.

"I hear you… and I believe you." She said it so low she almost didn't hear it herself.

Jacob turned his blank stare towards her. "What did you say?" he snapped. Did he assume she had said something else?

"I hear you and I believe you."

Jacob's steel grey eyes softened for a moment before his eyebrows furled as he appeared to dissect her words. He began to blink rapidly, and it looked as if he was blinking moisture from his eyes. The soft flicker of the lone candlelight didn't illuminate enough to be sure.

Lord soften his heart.

"Why?"

"What?" Shiloh stammered.

"Why do you believe me?"

Shiloh drew her knees up and wrapped her arms around them resting her chin on her knee.

"Well…you haven't given me a reason not to believe you."

Jacob held palms up as he pretended to showcase her prison.

Shiloh raised an eyebrow and smarted, "Well you didn't exactly lure me here with the promise of puppies or candy."

Jacob chuckled and plucked a beer off the plastic ring as if plucking a grape from the vine.

"Why do you do that?"

Jacob took a long gulp.

"What?"

"That." She nodded towards the can in his hand.

He looked at the beer for a while like he was reading the answer in the ingredients list before he shrugged.

"I don't know. Makes me feel better, I guess."

"Does it really? I mean… Don't you wake up with a hang over?"

"Not anymore," he chuckled.

"My dad used to drink. Said he was stressed out. Too much month at the end of the money. Wanna know what I learned from that?"

He raised an eyebrow.

"Hurt not transformed, often gets transmitted."

"What's that supposed to mean?" His face morphed into a mixture of insult and curiosity.

"It means, instead of using the pain of not being able to provide, fuel a passion to become more resourceful, he allowed that pain to inflict his family as well in more than one way."

He took another gulp.

Shiloh shrugged her shoulders. "My dad was amazing when he wasn't drinking. But that stuff was like the potion that turned Dr. Jekyll into Mr. Hyde."

"I believe that." He nodded.

"Then why do you do it?"

He ignored her until he emptied the can and started on another. "To deal with the past."

Shiloh had begun to nod off thinking the conversation was over. She sat up straight and cleared her throat. "I can understand that."

Lord, open his eyes and ears. Soften his heart and give me the words to say.

"But your past can either act as fuel or an extinguisher to your internal flame. It can either fuel you to become better or you can allow it to put the drive for life out completely. You decide."

"That's a nice analogy. But I'm afraid it's a day late and a dime short. My fire has been long put out." He tipped his can in her direction as if proclaiming a toast.

"As long as you're breathing it's not too late."

"Shouldn't you be begging for your freedom? Or better yet, your life?" he snarled as he lighted off the table in her direction. Shiloh didn't flinch as his face smashed into hers in an unwelcome kiss. He pulled back so the tip of their noses touched.

She looked into his once grey eyes now dilated to the point of completely black. She picked her hand up from the floor and placed it on his shoulder. He flinched at her gentle touch like a stray puppy does when pet for the first time. He studied her face while confusion painted his. What was she doing? She could quickly wrap the slack of her chain around his neck and once he was unconscious, she could be free. She knew where the key was. She could almost feel the warm steel key in her hand and hear the click of the Master Lock unbolting.

Ninety and nine.

A peace and an undeniable weight of forgiveness and love for the broken man in front of her flooded her soul at that moment. She no longer saw him as a monster that tortured her but pictured him as the abandoned and scared fifteen-year-old boy. His pain had not been transformed, he was still enduring it and was transmitting it like some horrible disease to all he touched.

"You're still breathing. You're not dead yet. You survived. Now thrive."

He sat back and his eyes returned to a soft grey. "H-How?" he stammered.

"The only way you can. Jesus."

He snorted. "You don't know what I've done. What I've done to you is nothing. What I've done to three others. This ain't my first rodeo." His eyes began to dilate again.

Father! Please!

"Don't you know of Saul who became Paul? He killed and imprisoned innumerable amount of people! You're mild in comparison."

"Did he take women?"

Frustration and bitterness began to cloud her mind. Paul didn't rape women… Maybe he was right. Maybe salvation wasn't for the vilest offender.

Ninety and nine.

Shiloh heard the old hymn and saw its poetic stanzas

played out like a movie in her head. Jesus was the Good Shepherd and she was the one sheep out of one hundred that went astray. Yet Jesus left the ninety and nine to come save her… to save Jacob.

"Not that scripture says, but King David, who is listed as a man after God's own heart, stole a man's wife and forced the husband to the front lines of battle to be killed."

He leaned forward listening with intent. "God still wanted him?"

"Yes. Do you have any children?"

He shook his head.

"Okay, hear me out. When my children mess up, they tend to hide and avoid me. That's our natural instinct when we mess up. We try to hide it or fix it ourselves, usually resulting in an even bigger mess. David did the same. He got the woman pregnant and instead of repenting for his adulterous behavior and going to God for forgiveness and help, he ends up sinning even more. Sin usually makes us do one of two things; run to God or run from God. When in reality, all God wants is for us to run to Him so He can help us fix it. Which leads to us trusting Him more and a stronger relationship with Him."

Jacob sat silent as he absorbed all she said. It was obvious he had never been presented with this truth. He chewed his lip.

"I want to be free."

"Ok… I can help you pray if you want."

He nodded.

"Father, we come to You now in repentance and seeking forgiveness for Jacob. Heal his heart, Lord. Transform his hurts so they can no longer be transmitted. Send your Spirit to fill him. In Jesus Christ's name. Amen."

"Amen."

Shiloh smiled wide as Jacob lifted his head and she hugged him tightly. Feelings of joy and victory overwhelmed her as thought of the freedom Jacob would now receive and possibly her own. Excitement at the thought of seeing her family again was deflated as she felt Jacob's body tense up and his tight grip on her wrist breaking her embrace. Startled she looked into his face. A face she hadn't seen in quite some time.

"No. Please. Please. Fight it!" she cried as he forced her onto the hard floor.

Fifteen

Shiloh awakened to the sound and stench of Jacob's retching filling the air. Her whole body ached as she searched for the words to say to him. She couldn't focus past the sharp pains shooting back and forth in her abdomen.

It had been so long since the last attack. Why did he do it now? Why did he have to pretend like he wanted forgiveness or God? Anger crept up her throat and she swallowed hard to push it back down. If mind games were what he wanted to play, she didn't want to give him any satisfaction.

I was tempted.

She closed her eyes tightly to try to hear the voice again, but Jacob's retching and gagging made it nearly impossible. Why was he throwing up? He hadn't had that much to drink.

I was tempted.

She remembered. She opened her eyes in time to meet his as he turned over and away from the area where his stomach contents flooded the floor.

"I told you… I'm too far gone." He wiped his mouth with the back of his hand.

"Yeah… maybe you are," she whispered as she choked back tears.

A proud look flashed across his face before anger and he flew into a kicking and punching fit. Shiloh turned over in an attempt to ignore him.

I was tempted.

She stopped and laid flat on her back instead, staring up at the ceiling.

"Jacob…" She pushed through clenched teeth.

He couldn't hear her over the sound of his fists colliding with the wooden wall or the rattling from the empty cans scattering across the floor.

"JACOB!" She sat up and shouted after him.

Her shout startled him out of his tantrum. The physical exertion it took to throw such a tantrum left him breathless and huffing for air.

"What?" he managed to exhale before gulping another breath as his eyes struggled to stay dilated.

"Alright, God. It's on You." She continued to stare past him.

"What?"

"Even Jesus was tempted."

"What in the hell does that have to do with me?"

"Because… just because you're tempted doesn't mean you're not saved. Even Jesus was tempted, it's what you DO with that temptation."

"You know what I just did." He wiped the sweat from his forehead and pulled a can of snuff from his pocket.

"Yeah… you let your temptation have the power to transform you into something you don't want to be."

"So how do I beat it?" he huffed as he shoved the can back into his pocket.

"Jesus."

"We tried that."

"No. No YOU didn't." She shook her head as she wiped the tears trickling down her cheeks.

He placed a plug inside his lip and avoided looking at her.

"Let your emotion become your testimony. When you're tempted, remember how Jesus has already delivered you from it. He has already set you free."

A loud noise interrupted her explanation. It was a sound that threw her into the past. What was it? A distant memory. It rang out three more times before she realized what it was, and Jacob pulled it from his pocket.

₞∛ℛ

Jacob fought another wave of nausea as he fumbled with the ringing phone in his pocket. Who would be calling him? He scanned the caller I.D., a familiar number but the owner's name hadn't been saved. He furled his eyebrows and placed a shushed finger over his lips. Shiloh nodded in obedience.

"Hello."

"Jacob?" the voice whispered. It took Jacob a moment to realize who it was. No wonder the number didn't have a name, it had been deleted.

"D-Delilah?"

"Yeah…"

Could this be it? Could she had finally come to her senses and left Blann? He glanced at Shiloh and his stomach twisted into knots. He'd have to do something with her, soon.

He tried to hear clearly what she was saying but her hushed tone and urgency in her cracking voice made it impossible.

"Slow down. I can't catch what you're sayin'."

"Do you have that girl?" She talked slow and low, but Jacob could picture her standing chest out and chin up fiddling with the cigarette resting between her fingers.

Jacob's eyes widened when his mind processed what she asked him, and a cloak of fear weighed on him. He hadn't felt fear since he found out Ma and Pops had been killed.

"You hear me?"

"Yeah..."

"Yeah you hear me or yeah you got her?"

Jacob's mind paced the room as his feet seemed cast in concrete.

"Your silence answers my question. You best get ou-"

Jacob hung up the phone and pulled the key to Shiloh's lock from his pocket.

"What? What's going on?" She could feel his panic and it became contagious.

"OW! You're hurting me." She flinched as he unwrapped the chain carelessly exposing her scabbed and scarred ankle's skin.

"Hurry up!" He pulled her to her feet.

"What's going on!" She tried to place weight in her heels and hold her place.

"Come on!" He began to drag her.

"Are you letting me go?"

He dragged her to his truck and threw her inside on the driver's side.

"Scoot over."

She scrambled to the passenger side

"What is going on?" Just then she heard the distant cries of police sirens.

෨ଓ

Shiloh pleaded with Jacob as fast as the speedometer on his truck rose. The distant wailing of sirens wasn't as distant anymore.

"Jacob. Please. Just pull over and let me out." She could see his pulse throbbing in his neck. It had to be the only thing in the world racing faster than his pickup.

"Please pull over. They'll stop for me and that'll give you time to get away."

His cheek jerked as he clenched his teeth. "Then they'll know I had you!"

"Please! Slow down then!" Bracing herself as the caution arrows began to appear as they started into a curve. The yellow signs were pulsating blue causing her to jerk around to see a line of flashing blue lights as far as she could see. This was it. She was going home, whether it be home to Harbor and the kids or home to Heaven, she didn't know.

"Jacob! PULL OVER!" She had tried reasoning with him to no avail which left her to use her assertive "mom" voice.

"SHUT UP! You want me to kill us both?!"

The smell of burning rubber and the strobing lights made her head throb.

Jacob's eyes were glued to the road unfolding before them. She couldn't get to him. He wouldn't listen. She began pleading to the One she knew would.

Father, Please. Please let us get out of this alive.

Jacob groaned an aggravated moan.

She glanced over at his speedometer; one hundred and nine. How was the calvary of cops behind them able to keep up? Squeezing her eyes tight. Jerking around, the smoke from the tires, and the flashing lights was hard enough to take. She didn't want to watch how the rest of this mess she was in would unfold.

The sound of rain began to fill her ears as it pelted the windshield and forced her to open her eyes. All the humidity in the air was evident of the storm that was to come, she had hoped it would hold off, but it hadn't and a storm it was.

Lips trembling, she cried out over the frantic wiping of the windshield. "Father, Please! Help us!"

A bolt of lightning drowned out the flashing police lights and slowed down time. She looked at Jacob's knuckles white on the steering wheel and his jaw set. His eyes were as wide as the can of chewing tobacco he kept in his pocket.

A boom of thunder shook the truck and sped time forward as another crack of lightning flashed in front of them.

She couldn't blink fast enough, as soon as the flash exploded in front of them so did the base of a tree, and as fast as the tree came down the back of the pickup came up and over the front.

Sixteen

"Get EMT!" Harris screamed into his radio clipped on his chest as he watched the full-sized truck flip, bumper over bumper. Each rotation landing before flying off the shoulder of the road like an Olympic gymnast. By the time it stopped its somersaults and stuck its landing, it no longer resembled a vehicle, much less a pickup.

The calvary of backup slowed their cruisers to a creep before each parked in front of the mangled mess of crumbled metal.

Harris tried to compose himself, but adrenaline had his entire body trembling. He jumped out of his cruiser. Crossing through the sea of debris, the undeniable scent of gasoline filled the air and an urgency set in. The chemicals and dust burned his eyes slowing him down.

"Can anybody hear me?" he coughed as he brought his elbow up to shield his breathing. The sound of ambulance's distant sirens was welcomed. "Can you hear me?"

A couple of his officers brought up the rear to assist.

"Hey, Harris!" Deputy Strickland nodded towards a small frame sprawled in the grass close to the tree line.

ৰাজ

The phone didn't even get a full ring out before Harbor answered it. He spit the nail he had just bit off as he spoke.

"Hello?"

"Mr. Romans."

"Yeah. Yeah. You got her?"

"Mr. Romans, there's been an accident and I'm gonna need you to come on to the Vaughn."

"Is she okay? Can we not send her to Jackson or Baptist East?"

"I'm afraid there might not be time."

Harbor let out a loud exhale as if someone had just kicked him in his chest. It took a minute to catch his breath, but his voice didn't return with it.

"Mr. Romans?"

"Yeah… I-I'm coming."

Standing in front of the triage room that Harris led him to, a doctor stepped out before Harbor had a chance to open the door, preventing him to enter.

"Are you her husband?"

He nodded.

"Mr. Romans… be brief." He offered a sympathetic nod before opening the door.

Shock froze him at the foot of the hospital bed. A blanket of sadness covered him as he studied his once lively, beautiful wife covered in bruises. Her forehead was stitched up and her lips looked as if they were turned inside out. The purple, blue, and black colorations around her eyes looked as if the girls had played makeup and overdid the eyeshadows. He tried to speak softly but choked on emotion. He cleared his throat to try again but uncontrollable tears ran down his cheeks and refused to fall alone. He stood there a sputtering mess.

This wasn't how it was supposed to happen. If she was to be found, she was to be dead or alive, not floating somewhere in between. God was proving Himself to be even more cruel than Harbor had thought.

The echoing drawn out beep of Shiloh's heart monitor flatlining pulled Harbor from slow motion and thrust him into fast forward as nurses whizzed by him, one pushing a table with a pair of chest paddles. The doctor who had open the triage door was now ordering for him to find it and use it. How he ended up on the other side of the door he couldn't remember but the door closed on the chaos and he stood alone in a quiet hall.

He trudged past the nurses' station and collapsed into a cold plastic seat. Burying his face into his hands, sobs racked his body and spilled over to the chair causing it to scratch against the floor. He hadn't prepared for this. His Shi, so close, yet so far away. Him present, but unable to save her. He looked at his hands wet with tears. What good were these hands? He could fix machines, lift babies, caress a woman, defend himself and others if need be, yet they couldn't do what he wanted more than life itself; heal Shiloh.

Come to Me, ye who are weary.

The scripture flashed in his mind. He was weary. He wanted, no, *needed,* rest. He glanced around the waiting room. The only company he had was an elderly man who slumped over in his seat, his nose whistling as he snored.

Harbor bowed his head.

"God… I'm sor-"

"Mr. Romans?"

Harbor snapped up.

"We've got her stable."

"Thank you. Can I-"

"No. No, we best let her rest. You may sit in but don't try to talk to her. Her brain needs to rest. She's been through a lot."

Harbor nodded.

ഇരുവ

Harris greeted the young deputy guarding the door to Jacob's hospital room before opening it and stepping inside. An older nurse stood by his I.V. tower pushing fluids into the saline bag.

"Here's a little something for the pain." She injected another syringe into the I.V. port on his wrist.

He deserves to feel all the pain.

Harris stared at Jacob in disbelief. Not a scratch anywhere that he could see. Only a few bruises. How was that possible? Both him and Shiloh should be dead, and the justice side of Harris believed Jacob should be the one fighting for his life, not Shiloh. Harris waited for the nurse to exit.

"Your rights have been read to you." Flipping his pocket notebook open he pulled the pen from his pocket. "I've got a few questions."

Jacob stared out the window avoiding eye contact. "I know my rights and I don't have anything to say without my lawyer."

"Okay. Do you have one or do you need one appointed to you?"

"I ain't got one."

Harris nodded. "There will be one appointed to you." He turned to walk out when Jacob piped up.

"Is she alive?"

Harris thought for a moment; he could use the idea of Shiloh as a witness to get him to talk. "Yeah, and she's talking."

Jacob squirmed in the bed and Harris left out with a smirk, a wave of satisfaction rushed over him. He made his way to the nurse's station.

"I need to see the doctor for Jacob Solomon."

"Okay. Let me page her."

"Thank you." Harris was scanning his notes when she walked up.

"Detective Harris?"

"Yeah, are you Mr. Solomon's doctor?"

She nodded.

"How long until he can be released?"

"Well, that's uncertain for now. We have to wait for the results from his scans and as long as they show nothing abnormal, he will be cleared."

"And how long until that?"

"Hopefully within the next few hours."

"Good. Thank you."

She smiled and excused herself. Harris went back to the deputy standing guard busy flirting with a red headed nurse.

"Hey. Focus."

The deputy snapped to attention as Harris walked up.

"Nobody comes in or out without a hospital name tag."

"You got it boss."

Seventeen

Jacob watched as the rain streamed down his room window. Why wasn't he dead? How come the tree fell just as soon as Shiloh cried out to God for help? Why didn't God answer his prayer for renewal?

Glancing around the room searching for something, he found the remote to the T.V. bolted to the wall. *Click.* Nothing. He turned it over and removing the backing he found out why it wouldn't power on. The batteries had been removed.

Leaning over, he pulled the bedside table open, no batteries, only a maroon book with gold lettering on the cover which read, Holy Bible. He slammed the drawer shut.

If God wouldn't listen to Shiloh's prayer for him, He didn't want to listen to anything Jacob had to say. Shiloh was good, he was not. There was no point in reading that book.

That none may perish, but that ALL would be saved.

He peered at the crack beneath the door. He glanced at the telephone beside his bed. He looked at the T.V. still black. Who had said that? He looked to the table beside him. Once again, he leaned over, opening the drawer, he pulled out the Bible. Setting it in his lap, he stared at it for a while before praying, as if he were talking to the book.

"Uh, God. If you're real, if this is real, make it real to me. Be my God like you are Shiloh's."

He opened it at random and he landed on John 18.

ഇരു

The vibrating phone in his pocket made him step out of Shiloh's room and into the busy hospital hall.

"Hello?"

"Hey, Harbor. How's she doing?"

"She's doing good. She's stable. Just waiting on her to wake up."

"That's good. What's the doctor saying?"

"Not much. Just that she'll wake up when she's ready. We're not going to rush it."

"Yeah. Well I don't think we're gonna need her to witness."

"No?"

"Nah. He won't be able to worm his way out of this one. Forensic evidence is strong."

"Good. I hope they stick him good."

"I'll keep you posted."

"Thanks, Harris."

"No problem."

Hanging up he tiptoed back into Shiloh's room where he found her as he had left her, except her eyelids were fluttering.

"Shi?" he whispered as not to startle her.

She blinked faster.

Harbor crept to the foot of the bed and caressed the top of her foot motionless under the blanket.

"Shi, can you hear me?"

She let out a low groan.

"Shi, babe, you're gonna be okay. I'm gonna take you home."

Tears welled in her eyes as she moved her lips as if she were talking, yet no sound accompanied it. Her eyes frantically scoped the room. Her chest heaved and her breathing became heavy.

"Shi, relax. Babe. You gotta relax."

He moved up beside her and took her hand. He studied her heart monitor startled at how it resembled the Appalachian mountain range. Each peak topping out higher and higher until alarms rang out and nurses rushed into the room. Harbor sprinted to the corner of the room watching wide-eyed as nurses pushed syringes of fluid into Shiloh's veins through her I.V. port. Everyone in the room could tell when the drugs began to take effect as Shiloh's groans became softer and her eyelids grew heavy.

"What happened?" Confusion crippled him.

"She's likely had some memory loss, it's common with concussions."

"She has amnesia?"

"No. She's probably just scared because she doesn't know how she ended up here." The nurse adjusted the drip on the saline bag.

"Oh, okay. How long will she be asleep?"

"Not too long. I didn't give her much. Just enough to take the edge off." The nurse scribbled something on Shiloh's chart before closing the door.

Harbor trudged back to his spot next to Shiloh's bed. He slumped down into the stiff hospital recliner and bowed his head.

"God, I've done wrong lately. I haven't been living right by You. I've been mad at you and instead of drawing near to You. I've run from You. I can't do it anymore. I can't do it anymore without You. Please Father, please, help Shiloh. Heal her mind and body."

The sound of nurses pushing carts and conversing outside the door of Shiloh's room woke Harbor from the sleep he attempted on the rickety cot. He sat up and rubbed his neck to massage away the crick.

"Hey, there."

He was in the middle of a yawn when the familiar voice interrupted him.

"Wh-" He jumped up and scrambled to Shiloh's bedside.

She chuckled. "It's nice to see you, too." She moved her hand to his.

"Oh, Babe…" Harbor's voice cracked as crying, he kissed her hand.

"How are the babies? Where are they?" She struggled trying to sit up.

"Don't move. Just try to relax. They are fine. Momma's got them."

She sighed and flinched at the jolt of pain the expression caused.

"Shi… I… I'm so sorry." He looked down at her bruised hand.

"Don't be. There's nothing you could've done."

"No. I shouldn't have let you leave."

Shiloh chuckled. "You really think you could've stopped me?"

A nurse entered in carrying in a breakfast tray.

"Mr. Romans, I have your breakfast. Oh! Well, hello there! How are you feeling, honey?" She sat the tray of food onto the rolling bedside table and stood beside Shiloh opposite of Harbor.

"I feel like I got hit by a truck." Shiloh attempted to crack a smile but cracked her scabbed lip instead.

"Careful now." The nurse pulled some gauze from the nightstand and dabbed Shiloh's lip. "You didn't get hit by one, you were thrown from one. And you're lucky to be alive."

"Not lucky. Blessed," Harbor corrected.

Eighteen

The hospital's tiled floor sent a chill through Jacob's cheek and down his spine as he peeked through the crack underneath the door to his room. A makeshift prison as his body healed with a guard standing outside preventing him from escape or anyone's entrance. He could hear the muffled voice of the deputy in the distance. Was he no longer standing guard? Jacob turned his head so that his ear could receive the noise from outside the room. Clearer, he heard the deputy's cool voice and a young woman's laughter.

Jacob stood and placed his hand on the handle, holding his breath he slowly turned it until he heard the lock disengage. Peeking out he could see the deputy at the nurse's station flirting with an attractive woman in purple scrubs.

He slinked around the corner and sprinted to the stairwell. He stood for a moment, looking through the small window on the door to see if anyone had followed him. Nothing. He began climbing the three flights of stairs to the ICU floor. Once there, he wished the deputy with a big mouth would've open a little wider, revealing a room number as he told the nurse who worked Jacob just what he had done and where Shiloh had ended up.

He peered through the wire-meshed glass pane, checking both sides of the hall before opening the door and stepping into it. The overpowering scent of alcohol burned his throat and the rhythmic hum of respirators and beeping of monitors filled his ears. A janitor pushing a cart full of cleaning supplies turned the corner forcing Jacob to hide behind a towering cart full of food trays. Looking past the food trays, he watched as the janitor pulled his name tag from his front pocket scanning it causing the heavy automated doors leading into the ICU to open. Sprinting, Jacob slithered through the doors just before they closed but not fast enough for his gown to make it through. The doors had a tight grip on the corner of his pale blue gown, refusing to let him go. He was frantic as he pulled on the gown when he caught a glimpse of a nurse through the windows on the doors, heading his way. He tried levering his body weight against the doors but to his surprise the gown refused to tear. He ducked as he heard her talking on the other side of the door. He had made it this far. He began to pull his arms out of the gown when the doors opened, releasing him. He fell to the ground and scurried behind the door.

"Hey, Angela."

"Yeah?" The nurse paused in the doorway.

"Can you come here a sec?"

"Yeah." She went back the way she came and the doors closed.

A sigh of relief escaped his lips and he walked sideways, back to the wall, until reaching the end of the hall. He watched and waited until the janitor turned another corner before he edged to the corner of the wall and looked down each hall lined with doors leading into the patient's room. *Which one?* He wondered how he was going to find her.

Just then a man stepped out of one of the doors. A nagging familiarity. But Jacob couldn't place him. Who was he? He looked so familiar. The man spoke to a passing nurse. His voice! It was him. It was the man holding the children during the press release. The man on the T.V. of the gas station pleading for his wife. It was Shiloh's husband.

The man fell behind the nurse as they made small talk and disappeared into a room housing various vending machines. Jacob hurried to the door he saw him come out of. Without knocking, he entered.

ഇരു

"That was fast. I thought you said you'd have to look for a vending machine?" Shiloh didn't look up as she spoke in between bites of baked chicken and mashed potatoes.

"I read the story of that Peter guy denying Jesus."

Shiloh's eyes became as wide as the plate in front of her and her skin just as white. She tried to let out a scream but choked on a bite of food. While she sat sputtering and attempting to clear her throat, Jacob continued.

"Did Jesus forgive him?"

"What?" She began mashing the nurse's button on her bed as discreet as she could.

"Did Jesus forgive him after Peter denied him?" Jacob shifted his weight from one foot to the other.

"Uh… Ye-Yes, Peter became a great preacher." She stopped mashing the button. "Why?" she asked.

"Because He knew Jesus and walked close to Him and still denied Him. Yet Jesus forgave Him. I thought maybe, if Jesus can forgive someone who knew Him personally and still managed to screw up. maybe there's hope for me, right?"

Shiloh shrugged her shoulders and cleared her throat. "I told you before, as long as there's breath in your lungs, there's hope." She smiled small.

Beep.

"Mrs. Romans, did you need something?" the nurse called over the room intercom.

Shiloh glanced from Jacob to the intercom.

Beep.

"Mrs. Romans?" the nurse asked again.

Shiloh hesitated before answering. "Uh, no, ma'am. I'm sorry. Must've hit it on accident."

Beep.

"No problem."

"I'm sorry, Shiloh. For what it's worth, I'm sorry…"

She stared at him.

"I'm going after God… If He'll have me."

She cocked her head as if she were thinking, "He will."

He smiled. It was the first time she had seen him smile like that. It was a genuine smile that glowed. Perhaps even, a godly glow.

"I'm not taking your word for it. I'm going after Him. I just had to know if He forgave Peter. And I wanted to tell you. I know you have prayed for me."

A code rang out over the intercom and strict instructions for patients, staff, and visitors to stay in the rooms. While the intercom began to repeat the instructions again, the door to Shiloh's room swung open and Detective Harris and Deputy Loverboy rushed in guns drawn.

Jacob thrust his hands into the air before the deputy forced his wrists behind his back, handcuffing him.

"You okay?" Harris glanced over at Shiloh.

"Yes, I'm fine. He was only coming to apologize."

She looked at Jacob offering him a sympathetic smile.

"Jacob, seek Him. I forgive you but when God forgives you, it's so freeing."

Harris and the deputy stared in disbelief as Jacob nodded.

"Come on, let's go." Harris kept the gun pointed to Jacob's back.

Nineteen

The nurse's knock on the door made Shiloh straighten up from slipping her feet into her sandals.

"Mrs. Romans, I just have your discharge papers."

"Yay, I mean, I love ya'll and all, but I think the cabin had better food." She was surprised at her own joke.

Before the nurse could respond the door swung open and Harbor toting Millie on his hip with the other three children trailing behind entered.

Giddy screams of, "Momma! Momma! Momma!" filled the room and the hall and possibly even the entire floor. Shiloh caught Millie just as she leapt from Harbor's arms. Tears of happiness blinded her, but she kissed each head that bobbed in front of her.

"Oh! Oh! My babies! I've missed y'all so much! Oh, I love ya'll so much!"

The whole family became one big lump in the doorway of the room. Shiloh thought her heart would explode. When she finally was able to clear her eyes enough to see, all of them were crying, even the nurse. Shiloh laughed and attempted to stand and retrieve the papers and listen to further instructions but the children each had their arms wrapped around her neck, arms, and torso.

"I'm sorry," she giggled. "I promise I'm listening." Junior planted another tear stained kiss on her cheek.

"Ya'll are perfectly fine." The nurse smiled sweetly before she began down the list of dos and don'ts.

Shiloh continued receiving kisses and squeezes from her children until the nurse finished and Harbor took the papers.

"Alright, ya'll. Let's take Momma home."

The children cheered as if Harbor had just announced they were going for ice cream.

Shiloh fidgeted with the seat belt as a broad smile broke out across her face at the sight of the *Welcome Home* banner on the front porch. The children bounced back and forth in their seats like racehorses at the starting line of the Kentucky Derby. Instead of anticipating the firing of a revolver, they awaited the dying of the engine. As soon as Harbor killed the motor the children scrambled out of the car.

Ann left her siblings behind and snatched Shiloh's door open. "Momma! I've missed you so much!"

Shiloh barely made it out of the car before the rest of the children made it to her, burying their small faces into her. Each of them squealing with happiness until the younger two began arguing over who missed her more.

"Okay. Okay. That's enough. Let your Momma get inside out of the heat," Harbor said as he pried Junior off of her leg.

Shiloh laughed as she kissed each of their heads before picking up Millie.

"Momma, where have you been?"

"Millie, no, ma'am." Harbor shook his head

disapprovingly.

"Oh, Harbor. She's just a baby. She don't know any better." Shiloh rolled her eyes and snuggled into Millie's neck causing her to giggle.

Ann and Nora each kept an arm wrapped around Shiloh's waist as they all made their way through the yard, swarming with familiar pets, and into the house. Shiloh was so glad to see those annoying chickens again.

"Wow. I'm impressed," she teased as she looked around the Southern Homes & Gardens worthy living room.

"Hey, now. You have no faith in us?" Harbor scoffed. She laughed.

"Geez. Thanks."

"For real. Who did it?" She attempted to set Millie down who refused and drew her legs up.

"Hey… I'm hur-."

"Emily helped." Ann cut Harbor off.

Shiloh raised an eyebrow. "Emily?"

"Emily Sisters. She called whenever she heard. Wanted to know how she could help." He avoided eye contact as he sat in his recliner.

"Really? That was so sweet of her."

Just then, Deputy strolled into the room and sniffed at Shiloh before climbing onto the couch beside her and letting out a sigh.

"Well, it's good to see you too, Dep," she snickered patting his greying head. The memory of the blood curdling yelp Nino had let out made her stomach quiver. She inhaled deeply before exhaling. She turned towards Harbor and chewed her lip. She needed to know but didn't want to. Before she could ask, a squeaking sound down the hall caught her attention.

"Oh! Nino!" She ran towards him, startling him, he paused before trying to turn and run away. His frantic movements were more than his doggy wheelchair could take, resulting in him tipping over.

"Oh, Nino. My sweet boy! You're not dead!" Tears of happiness bubbled up as she picked him up, setting him upright. Sniffing her, he began licking and whining.

"I see where I rank. I didn't get a welcome like that," Harbor poked as Shiloh and the kids played with Nino just like before the accident.

"Yeah. You whine differently than he does. Yours is more annoying," she snapped.

"Yep, she's back," he snickered as he relaxed into his recliner.

৲〇৩

"This is good. You have no witnesses to testify against you as of right now." Mrs. Lyles dug in her briefcase as Jacob sat chained to the chair.

"What do you mean?"

"Mrs. Romans doesn't want to testify."

He kept his eyes down at the grey slippers the jail provided him at booking.

Detective Harris entered the block interrogation room. He laid his legal notepad and a manilla folder onto the table as he took his seat across from Jacob. "Mr. Solomon, I assume you met your attorney, Mrs. Lyles. I just want to ask you a few questions."

Mrs. Lyles leaned over and whispered into Jacob's ear. "Say nothing. I'll handle it."

Jacob nodded, eyes down, counting the stitches on his slippers.

"Where were you the morning of April 22nd?"

Jacob shrugged and looked to Mrs. Lyles for an answer.

"Maybe I can help jog your memory." Harris pulled some blown up pictures with the date and time in the corner of the frame and slid them across the desk to Jacob.

"That's your truck." He slid another picture.

Jacob recognized his blue Dodge Ram, but that truck was nothing special, there could be thousands just like it.

"And that's you." Harris slid the last picture which was a zoomed in shot of his face.

Mrs. Lyles glanced from Harris to the pictures to Jacob and back again to Harris.

"I-I didn't know of this. This is new evidence and I'm going to need to have a word with my client."

"You might want to know this other evidence as well," Harris replied coolly as he rose from his seat. "We got Mr. Solomon's DNA from the rape kit done on our victim and tested it against the DNA found on the three bodies dumped at various wooded areas… It was a match."

The lock engaging as Harris shut the door might as well have been the flipping of the switch to the electric chair. They were gonna fry him.

"Where you gonna put him?" Strickland asked.

"C block," Harris replied.

"But the only cell available is with Garcia."

"Exactly."

∞☙

Jacob stood in front of the steel door marked 22C in chipped black paint.

"Home, sweet home," the overweight guard said as he

unlocked it and ushered Jacob inside the small cell furnished with metal bunk bed and lone steel toilet that doubled as a sink.

He could tell the top bunk belonged to another inmate by the pictures taped on the wall beside the pillow.

Clank.

The sound of the heavy door closing behind, shook him. He took the sheets provided at booking and began making his bed when he heard the door open again. He glanced over his shoulder expecting to see the guard but was met with dark eyes that were set back inside a head the size of a bowling ball.

Jacob had no desire for small talk, all the interrogations left him mentally and physical exhausted. He could feel his cellmate's stare boring into his back as he finished making his bed and stretched out on it.

Twenty

Adjusting back into everyday life proved difficult. Shiloh's inner fire no longer blazed, warming the cold and shining light into darkness, it had waned dull leaving her a shell resembling the woman of former. Shiloh didn't ramble on about Heaven or spout out questions as fast as they shot across her mind. Her singing didn't enter the room long before her body anymore, she entered silently and seemingly vanished instead of visibly exiting. Living with her was not how Harbor remembered or hoped for at her return, she was plagued with anxiety and she became as a growth on Harbor's side. Where she was once stubbornly independent, she had returned sheepishly needy.

Harbor didn't mind it. He loved her and knew she loved him though she wasn't ready to intimately show him; he knew to a certain extent the trauma his beloved wife suffered those long months at the hands of her abductor, but most of the details of the trauma Shiloh only discussed with the detectives. Harbor wouldn't push her. He would wait as long as she needed.

What grated Harbor more than Shiloh's fire being put out was Shiloh's tenderness and compassion towards her abductor. Through all the questioning and pre-trial meetings Shiloh never allowed the evil done to her to guide her words or actions.

"An eye for an eye, Shi!" Harbor hissed just below the lawyer's earshot.

"Vengeance is mine saith the Lord," Shiloh would reply without hesitation or breaking her forward gaze.

Harbor couldn't argue Scripture with his wife. She was a walking Bible, well versed and had one readily available for each situation, more so since her disappearance.

What happened there? Harbor often found himself wondering while watching his wife's facial expressions change signaling a war inside. *Let him hang!* Harbor couldn't figure out why his wife protected her perpetrator.

"Shiloh, he's a monster." Harbor held her by her shoulders, forcing her to look into his eyes.

Shiloh's eyes filled with tears as she fought with her natural self who wanted nothing more than to punish Jacob. But her faith and her conviction wouldn't allow it. "Be not overcome with evil, but overcome evil with good."

"That doesn't mean to shut your eyes to evil and let the guilty walk!" Harbor replied through clenched teeth as he let his arms fall to his sides.

"No, it doesn't. I'm not trying to prevent justice. There are always consequences to one's actions. Good and bad. Jacob has earned jail time, no doubt about that. But I don't feel the death penalty is the way to go, either. Jacob repented," Shiloh explained as she and Harbor passed in between cars in the courthouse parking lot *en route* to their own.

Harbor reached the SUV first and opened Shiloh's door. "How are you so forgiving?"

"Because I'm forgiven." Shiloh smiled faintly and a tender love filled her eyes.

Harbor felt a pricking of his conscience and a small wave of envy. Anger was something that he struggled with daily, seemingly moment by moment. How he longed to have the charity that his wife possessed. The unity with her Lord, the same Lord he worshipped and loved.

"Well tomorrow we will see his fate," he sighed in defeat as he shut her car door.

Harbor locked the bedroom door behind him as he came in. Shiloh reading on her side of the bed was a sight that he had taken for granted before, but he was sure he'd never do it again. Climbing into bed next to her he pulled her close and nuzzled her neck.

"Harbor!" she giggled. "I'm trying to read." She kissed his forearm draped across her chest.

"You can read later… I've missed you." He kissed her neck, the scent of vanilla and coconut on her skin drove him wild. He kissed her again and he could sense her pulse quickening by the throbbing he felt with each kiss on her neck.

"I love you," he breathed heavy into her ear. She let her book fall to the side of the bed and pulled him closer. The blood roaring in his ears almost drowned out her whispers. He couldn't understand her. He continued kissing her and began to run his hand up her thigh when he felt her stiffen. He pulled away. "What's wrong?"

Her eyes were closed tight and her jaw, clenched.

"Shi? Babe?" He sat up.

Tears escaped from underneath her closed lids.

"Shi…" He didn't know what to do. He was afraid to touch her for fear she'd take it the wrong way. After what seemed as an eternity, she opened her eyes and turned towards him, tears still falling but slowing to a trickle.

"I'm sorry, Harbor." She shook her head.

"No, Babe, don't be. It's okay. I'm sorry… I just thought…" He rubbed the back of his neck.

"I know. I thought so, too… But I don't guess I'm ready yet."

They laid down and he stared at the ceiling attempting to count the bumps on the popcorn ceiling. He lost count after two hundred.

"Shi?"

"Yeah?" she mumbled sleepily.

"How long do you think it'll take?"

"I don't know. How long are you willing to wait?" She leaned up, blinking the sleep from her eyes.

He pulled her close. "As long as it takes."

She rested her head on his chest.

"But it has been almost six months."

She slapped his chest. "Shut up!"

They laughed for a while before each were lost in their own thoughts.

Harbor broke the silence. "Tomorrow's the day. You ready?"

"I'm ready for it to be a thing of the past. A part of my testimony."

He kissed her atop her head. "How's your headache?"

"Honestly? I don't know if it's gotten better or if I have gotten used to it." She sighed as she wrapped her arm around his waist.

He pushed her off, sitting up to look her in the eyes. "You're going to the doctor."

"Ugh. I've had my fill of hospitals and poking and prodding." She shrugged him off.

"Shiloh, you're going. Ain't no telling what you picked up in there."

She rolled her doe-brown eyes.

"You're going if I gotta throw you over my shoulder and take you."

"Fine," she huffed and settled back into his chest. Harbor kissed her head as both closed their eyes for a good night's sleep.

Sleep didn't come for Harbor, he tossed to and fro at the vivid nightmares that played like a bad movie he couldn't turn off. He stood before a tall judge's bench that reached into the clouds, he couldn't see who filled it. It wasn't like the homely cedar stained bench at the courthouse, it was majestic white marble with glittering slits of gold.

A terrifying voice called out his name, "Harbor Romans, you stand guilty of these charges, bearing false witness, covetousness, slander, idolatry, fornication, adultery, blasphemy…" A lengthy tattered scroll unraveled somewhere from the clouds; Harbor knew it came from the Judge. The scroll seemed endless as it rolled past Harbor into oblivion, sins committed in ignorance and knowingly alike with the date scribbled beside the offenses indicated he was only twelve. Harbor's heart sank to his stomach and his knees trembled. His voice shook as he tried to plead his defense.

"My sins have been forgiven by the Lord of my life, my Savior, Jesus Christ." He could barely hear himself as he whispered in terror.

"Judge and ye shall be judged," the voice boomed.

The magnitude of the voice forced Harbor to his knees and tears stung his eyes as he professed his faith again.

"Your honor, my sins have been forgiven by the Lord of my life, my Savior, Jesus Christ."

"JUDGE AND YE SHALL BE JUDGED!" Louder to the point of almost bursting Harbor's eardrums.

Melting to the floor beneath him, Harbor laid flat on his face and wept bitterly.

"Please… my sins are forgiven. I confessed Jesus and have lived since that day for Him."

"Walk worthy of the vocation in which ye are called, with lowliness, meekness, with long-suffering, FORBEARING ONE ANOTHER IN LOVE; endeavoring to keep the unity of the Spirit in the bond of peace. There is ONE body, and ONE Spirit, even as ye are called in one hope of your calling, ONE Lord, ONE faith, ONE baptism, ONE God and Father of all who is above all, and through all, and in you all. But unto everyone of you is given grace according to the measure of the gift of Christ."

Harbor drank in His Words and Harbor felt that which he longed for: charity.

"Jacob is forgiven."

He smiled as he acknowledged the truth and the scroll rolled up as quickly as it had unraveled before him.

৵৹৻৶

"Harbor?" Shiloh stared through the dark at her husband's face. The glow from the alarm clock shone a dull beam on his face causing the tears to glisten that crept out of the corner of sleeping eyes. She saw a faint smile emerge when Harbor's furrowed brow and tight lips softened.

"Harbor." Shiloh gently shook his shoulder, "You alright?"

Harbor opened his eyes, blinking away the tears and sleep, his voice cracked. "He's forgiven. I forgive him."

"Praise the Lord!" Shiloh hugged his neck and snuggled in close.

Twenty-One

The sound of thumping and a stinging pain radiating from his right cheekbone jerked Jacob awake. He opened his eyes just in time to see the foot coming to make contact yet again. He reacted quick enough to dodge the blow. He sat up as far as the overhead bunk would allow and tried to swing at the torso attached to the foot that was kicking him. His cellmate drug Jacob from his bunk and threw him onto the floor. Jacob tried to get to his feet but sleep and continual licks from his cellmate kept him down.

"What the hell, man?" Jacob scrambled on the cold concrete floor.

"You like beating up on women, huh? How you like it now?" His cellmate picked him up and threw him against the cinder block wall.

Jacob was able to get free with an uppercut to his chin.

The lights flickered on and three guards flooded the small cell.

"What's going on in here? Ya'll break it up."

"I ain't done nothing. I was asleep and he started kicking me." Jacob stared through his swollen eyes at his cellmate who held his chin.

"I don't like no woman beater, boss. You know that."

The guard nodded his head. "I know, Garcia, but you know the drill. Solitude."

The two other guards led Garcia out and the guard that he had referred to as boss turned to Jacob.

"You're lucky. Usually we get here too late."

∞⟨⟩∞

The jury was dismissed to converse, and the judge looked to Jacob.

"Do you have anything to say for yourself?"

He nodded at the judge, trying to find the words to say. Tears began to fill his eyes as he turned to look at the victim's families who filled the benches behind him. They didn't have to speak he had felt their presence. Their stares boring holes into the back of his close shaved head. He studied their faces, each filled with such hate, rightly so he thought; he hated himself, too. He no longer saw those women he had killed as worthless pigs but precious princesses. He continued down the line of hateful faces, choking on sobs and apologies until he reached Shiloh.

∞⟨⟩∞

Shiloh's stomach rose further into her throat as Jacob's gaze and apologies drew closer until finally resting on her.

Father, give me strength and add your super to my natural, giving me supernatural mercy and love for him. Let me see him as a brother and no longer a monster.

A warming peace fell on her as if the sunlight broke through the cold brick walls and warmed her skin instigating a peaceful smile. Tears of compassion rimmed her eyes as they locked with Jacob's. She knew he was forgiven, and this was one of many tests and trials that were to come as God used them to sanctify His chosen. She pitied Jacob for when she had become a babe in Christ, there were many who took turns feeding her the spiritual milk until she grew enough to feed herself and to feed on spiritual meat. Who was going to minister to Jacob in prison?

I take care of my flock.

Jacob's eyes were no longer a cold gray but had morphed into a soft hazel. She wanted to encourage him. To hug him and tell him not to worry, God would provide. She felt the hate radiating from the families seated beside her. They didn't know of the softening of his heart. Would they even care? Had it not been for Jesus' work in her own life, she wouldn't have either.

"I'm so sorry for what I did to you." He offered her the same apology he had offered her in the hospital.

Harbor squeezed her hand in support.

Shiloh still had a faint smile turning up the corners of her pale pink lips. Where the other hurt families permeated hate, Shiloh had a soft glow about her, one that shone hope, mercy, even love.

She nodded at his apology where the others had shaken their heads. She prayed God would grant them the freedom that came with forgiveness. Holding onto the weight of their hurt and hate was only going to pull them into Hell. Her heart hurt for them and she praised God for her release; physical and spiritual.

Jacob reclaimed his seat as the judge looked to the victims' bench.

"Do the families of the victims have anything they'd like to say?"

One after one, the families took to the stand condemning Jacob.

"I hope you get it as hard as you gave it.", "Go to Hell.", and "Rot in Hell." And a variety of phrases that all meant the same thing. "You can't be forgiven. You are evil."

Harbor accompanied Shiloh to the stand and stood behind her with his hand on her lower back. It was his way of offering support, emotionally and physically, if she needed it. The dream from the night prior was still fresh on his mind. His spirit wrestling with his nature, he began to speak.

"Jacob… I forgive you and I'll be praying for you," he said quickly, not trusting his fleshly nature to take over and add to the list of damnations Jacob had already received.

The courtroom erupted in gasps and murmurings causing the judge to pound his gavel three times.

"Order, Order in the court."

He turned towards Shiloh asking, "Do you have anything you'd like to say, Mrs. Romans?"

She nodded.

Father give me the words to encourage this baby of Yours.

She looked to Jacob, it seemed as if he had shrunk a little lower under each verbal attack, she could easily deliver the final blow, crushing him entirely. "Jacob…"

He perked up at the soft tone of her voice reminding Shiloh of how a flower perks up at the first raindrop after a drought.

"Do you know what Jacob means?"

He nodded. "Deceiver."

Surprised, she nodded. "Yes. But do you know what Jake means?"

Confused, he shook his head.

Shiloh smiled, "Forgiven."

He sent her a blank look.

"You will no longer be called Jacob, you are no longer a deceived man of the world, but you are now Jake, a forgiven child of God."

Jake dropped his head on the table in front of him and spread his arms towards Heaven and wept bitter sobs that shook his body.

Shiloh and Harbor stepped down and walked through the courtroom filled with chaos and kept walking, eyes forward, until they reached their truck.

ഇൻ

Crack, crack, crack.

The hard-browed judge banged his gavel on its designated spot. "Court is back in session. Has the Jury reached a verdict?"

"We have your honor." A slender black lady in a plum purple pant suit rose from her seat.

"We, the jury, find the defendant guilty of three counts of capital murder, four counts of sexual torture, four counts of rape in the first degree, four counts of sexual abuse in the first degree, one count of kidnapping, and one count of unlawful imprisonment. We the jury suggest a sentence of life imprisonment." The lady in the plum pant suit nodded towards the victim's families.

The judge observed Jacob over the rim of his bifocals. "Well, Mr. Solomon, the jury has made their suggestion and with all due respect…" He nodded at the jurors who sat to his left. "In the state of Alabama, a judge has the authority to impose the death penalty against the jury's verdict in favor of life imprisonment. And I, being of sound mind, the reviewing of this case and the sheer brutality you inflicted upon your victims, understand that you have declared that you clearly cannot live among us and certainly do not deserve to live at all, I sentence you to death by lethal injection."

Though his life had just been decided for him, he had such a joy. He was a new creation in Christ. He wanted to shout it from the rooftops. But he also felt such remorse for the victims' families and did not want to rub salt in their gaping wounds, wounds that he caused.

Twenty-Two

When they got into their truck, Harbor patted Shiloh's frail hand that rested on the center console. She slumped in the seat, exhaustion swept over her, or was it the supernatural power leaving her?

"Stop at the gas station and get me a Goody powder, please," she said rubbing her temples.

Harbor looked at the clock on the dash. "It's only ten past two. Let's take you on to the doctor real quick."

"UGH," she groaned. She was exhausted. Fatigue and headaches were her constant companions. She knew there was no point in arguing with Harbor. He had already made plans and had the kids scheduled to go to his mother's after school. "Fine. But stop and get me a Goody powder first. I'm not sitting in a doctor's office all afternoon with a splitting headache."

Harbor grinned, his spunky, spitfire of a wife slowly emerging from the ashes.

When arriving at the doctor's office, they were greeted by a courteous nurse and the all too familiar sterile scent of alcohol. Shiloh's headache pulsated at the smell and she prayed that God would quicken the effects of the medicine.

She filled out the sign-in sheets and took a seat next to Harbor. The room was small with only twelve chairs and a T.V. mounted on the wall. Medical Certificates and charts lined the floral wallpaper and one of the corner areas was occupied by toys and children's books. A pregnant woman and her husband waited their turn to be called as their daughter who looked to be about three, took interest in a book about mermaids.

Harbor gave a knowing smile and nodded at the couple. "You miss that?"

He asked Shiloh under his breath as the very pregnant woman wrestled the book from her daughter to keep her from licking the bright pictures that filled it. Shiloh snickered.

"Awe, Momma. But it looks so tasty!" she teased the mother in an attempt to ease her embarrassment.

"Right?" The woman appreciated the gesture.

"We have four. I know how it is." Shiloh leaned her head back against the wall behind her and closed her eyes, trying to stop the pounding in her head.

"WOW!" the couple exclaimed.

Harbor grinned, nodding his head.

The nurse came out and called the small family back, leaving Shiloh and Harbor sitting in silence for about ten minutes.

"Shiloh Romans?"

Shiloh and Harbor fell in line behind the nurse as she led them to their room which resembled a cubicle. In the corner, an examination table overlaid with paper and a thin pillow sat crookedly at the top. More medical posters which looked to be from the eighties were taped to the walls to give the patient reading material. One chair, looked have been placed in there at the same time as the posters, was pushed up into a small opening between the examination table and a counter which held multiple clear canisters filled with all type of basic medical supplies.

As she took her place atop the table, Harbor squeezed in between the tight opening to take the vacant chair. Once seated, he crossed his arms in an attempt to gain more space.

The nurse entered again with a digital scale in hand this time. "Mrs. Romans, let me get your weight." One hundred and five. She had gained nearly fifteen pounds since coming back home. It was a welcomed number.

"Okay, sweetie. You can have a seat." The older nurse scribbled her weight onto her chart. "So, what brings you in today?"

"I've been having bad headaches."

"Okay. Any change in diet, household cleaners, environment?"

Shiloh didn't want to speak of the cabin. She wanted to close off that part of her life just as she had let the doors of the courtroom close behind her. She paused before she pressed forward.

"Yes ma'am. I was held captive for a little over three months in an old, rotting cabin."

An expression of shock accompanied her tender voice. "Oh, sweetie. I'm so sorry."

Shiloh could tell the woman wanted to hug her but chose against it, only shaking her head as her eyes became glossy. The grey-haired nurse meant well, but Shiloh hated it. She hated the pity. It reminded her of the way people looked at her and her siblings when they showed up at school in tattered clothes and dingy shoes.

"It's okay. I'm okay. God is gracious!" She replied softly.

He's just not always fair.

The thought flew across her mind quicker than she could hold it captive.

The nurse continued down the usual list of questions.

"Are you taking anything?"

"Yes ma'am. I take 25mg of sertraline daily for depression."

"Do you think you may be pregnant?"

"No, ma'am. He's had a vasectomy." She nodded towards Harbor.

A ping of remorse hit Harbor at the remembrance of why he had gone through with the procedure.

"Besides, I'd be puking up my guts if I was. Shoot, from the moment of conception until delivery, I'd be barfing." She laughed then grimaced as a sharp pain shot across her forehead from her left temple. She sat quiet as she rubbed it while Harbor and the nurse chuckled at her humor.

She appreciated it as it seemed to lift the fog of remorse and pity. She peeked out of the corner of her eye to catch a glimpse of Harbor's smile as he laughed. Feelings of love and affection washed over her at the sight of it. She loved making him laugh.

"Okay, Sweetie. We're gonna get some blood and run some tests and the doctor will be in shortly."

"Yes, ma'am."

After waiting long enough to study the posters repeatedly, Shiloh was sure she could identify symptoms of measles, scarlet fever, chicken pox, and a slew of other illnesses before a rapping on the door followed by the doctor entering in, chart in hand.

"Good evening! How are y'all?" He was loud and boisterous, no doubt the life of the party in his heyday, now long behind him as he appeared to be in his mid-seventies.

Shiloh smiled. "To be honest, a lot better if I wasn't here."

He laughed hearty. "Yeah, I believe so! I'm Dr. Brown." He leaned against the counter after laying the chart down and crossing his arms. "We got the results and you definitely need to take some iron supplements because you're anemic."

"That's it?" she snorted. "I've been anemic for forever and I've never suffered from headaches like this."

He shook his head. "No. No. No. I'm not done. Let me finish." He pumped his hand as if he were pumping brakes.

"No, after looking over everything, your iron and your blood pressure aren't the only thing that's a little concerning."

Harbor and Shiloh both squirmed in their seats. Anticipation wasn't a welcomed emotion. Had he not read the nurse's notes?

His demeanor changed from jovial to confused as he told them what he had assumed they had already knew.

"Without further testing or scans, of course, but I'm convinced that your pregnancy is the cause of your headaches."

Shiloh stared past him. What had he just said? The headache must've affected her hearing. She couldn't have heard him correctly. Harbor beat her to it before she could ask him to repeat it.

"What?" Harbor stood.

Confusion painted Dr. Brown's face as his eyes

jumped from Harbor to Shiloh.

"She's pregnant."

Shiloh could feel Harbor staring at her. She avoided his gaze keeping her eyes fast on Dr. Brown who squirmed uncomfortably in front of her. She tried to reason within herself but couldn't.

"How could this have happened?" She felt her eyes begin to sting.

Dr. Brown still confused, she explained what she meant.

"I have been in captivity for months… After the first month, I didn't have a period."

Dr. Brown furled his eyebrows and opened her chart, obviously reading the nurses notes for the first time as his face softened and confusion turned to compassion. He closed the folder and scratched his greying head then tried laying down his hair.

"I'm so sorry, ya'll. I had no idea."

"How could this happen?" Harbor persisted through clenched teeth.

"Well… usually if a body is lacking proper nourishment the first thing to go is anything that forces the body to exert extra energy. For a female, that's her menstrual cycle. It doesn't mean she cannot get pregnant, though." His eyes and voice were soft as he explained.

Shiloh dropped her face into her hands. She felt as she had when she had found out she was pregnant at seventeen. Fear and shame consumed her. A tender touch on her shoulder made her look up, hoping it was Harbor's made the burden of fear and shame heavier at the realization that Dr. Brown had come over to console her and Harbor still stood stoic at her side.

"Mrs. Romans… If you want… I can have my nurse

make you an appointment at Planned Parenthood.”

Shiloh's stomach turned. Images of aborted babies and the video of the abortion procedure she had played so many times for the clients at the crisis pregnancy center she volunteered at before her abduction flashed in her mind.

“NO. Absolutely not.”

Harbor had beat her to it again. A feeling of relief quickly dissipated as she looked to Harbor standing sternly and avoiding eye contact. The room and her womb were filled, but she felt a crippling loneliness.

Once in the privacy of their truck, Shiloh addressed the tension that filled the void of words. “I'm not sold on continuing this pregnancy.” She stared out the window watching the city fade into countryside.

“What do you mean, you ain't sold on it? You're pregnant. The blood tests confirmed it.”

A ball of anger began to rise from her stomach and seemed to lodge in her throat. She tried hard to swallow it and when she couldn't get it down, she let it out. “I know what the test said. I was in there. I'm not stupid.” She looked at his knuckles white on the steering wheel. “I'm not sold on going through with this pregnancy.” She watched him waiting for a response.

His cheek jerked.

“What the hell do you mean, Shi? You just gonna go abort it? That's not gonna make it better. If anything, that'd make it worse.” His voice rose with the tension that filled the cab.

“No. But I sure don't see how it could help matters. Think about the kids. They've been through enough already. Me being gone and then all of a sudden I'm back, but oh, wait now kids don't get too comfortable because in a few months your world's gonna be turned upside down again with a new baby." She mimicked his sarcasm and volume. "And another thing. It's MY body that's going to have to go through all the stress a pregnancy puts on, not to mention all the stares and questions of our neighbors I will be forced to endure." Bitter tears began to roll down her cheeks.

"So, that's what it's about then. It's what will everyone else think and feel."

"Yeah. Yeah it is. Think about this long and hard, Harbor. I mean really think before you answer me. No knee-jerk response that you've been instructed."

He cut his eyes at her insinuation of not being able to think for himself. "What," he said through clenched teeth.

"Would you be able to love Jacob's child as your own? Could you look Jacob in the face and kiss his cheeks? Bounce him on your lap? Let him drive in the mixer trucks with you? Because there's a fifty-fifty chance that the baby would look like him."

He began to answer but she held her hand up.

"Uh-uh. I'm not done. Would you be able to love me? You told me the first time I ever nursed Ann in the hospital, that it was the most beautiful thing you'd ever seen. Would you feel the same way with Jacob's baby? Would you allow that baby to sleep in between us like our own babies did? Would you be able to love me while I loved on Jacob's baby? This isn't some lifetime movie, Harbor. This is real life and emotions aren't scripted."

She stared at him awaiting his response and when it looked as if there wouldn't be one, she turned her attention back to the trees flashing by until they pulled into the driveway of her mother-in-law's house. He put it in park and placed his hand on her thigh.

"I think you're worrying too much about what everyone else thinks and not nearly enough about what God thinks."

She pushed his hand off her leg.

Twenty-Three

Days of cold shoulders and silent treatment between Shiloh and Harbor and after much ruckus from the rowdy kids, she had to find an excuse to escape. Funny, she never would have guessed she would crave the silence. Especially not since she had spent nearly four months surrounded by silence.

"I'm gonna run and grab some milk, okay?"

Harbor looked up from his phone perplexed and nodded slow as obvious confusion bound his tongue.

She shuffled out of the clamoring house, leaving behind Millie and Junior chasing the wheelchair ridden pug and the two older girls arguing over which outfit the baby doll they were playing with should wear.

She exhaled when she was safe within the confines of her truck. Had she held her breath the whole time? Being alone had born something she assumed she would loathe, but instead of abhorring it, she sipped it long and slow like a fine wine. In the three months she was abducted she had become as dependent on solitude as an alcoholic is its bottle. Hating it but driving mad without it. She had lived with crickets chirping as her constant feed and the

166

replacing of it with children chiding wasn't a simple adjustment.

Shiloh drove until she arrived at the abandoned parking lot of a former drug store. After parking, she watched as the cars whizzed past. She wondered how many of the people racing by even noticed her, sitting motionless and watching them. She wondered how long Jacob had sat watching her. She shivered and turned her A.C. down, knowing full well that the shiver wasn't due to some physical discomfort, but a mental.

She frowned as she looked down at her pudge. A physical reminder of what she'd been through. She thought about the remarks and opinions of church members and the apprehensions of family on her pregnancy. Majority of them telling her to think of her mental health and her family's. Was Harbor wrong for thinking having this baby was the right thing to do? Her whole family dynamic was about to change. Could Harbor love the baby as if it were his own? Could she? There was always the option of adoption. But she and Harbor themselves had talked about adopting in the future and yet, here she was pregnant after they had assumed pregnancy was no longer in the cards. Some even went to the extent that it was her body and it wasn't consensual, so abortion was "permissible."

Be not overcome of evil, but overcome evil with good.

The verse rang out in her mind. Two wrongs didn't make a right. She couldn't abort. God had entrusted her with this baby. He had allowed her womb to open just as she was about to go home. Back to a house, healthy food, and a loving family. She was going to view this baby just as she viewed her others. This was a responsibility that God had trusted her with. What Satan meant to use to mess her and her family up, she would allow God to use as a message. She was going to choose love. She was going to choose life.

Just then a familiar feeling in her abdomen she had once thought she would never feel again: the fluttering of a baby's kicks.

₞ℓ

"I spoke to Emily on the phone today."

Harbor stiffened a little at Emily's name.

"Yeah?" He spat his toothpaste into the sink.

"Yeah, I invited her over for dinner tomorrow night. I figured we'd grill some of your famous chicken." She spoke as she flipped through the pages of her Bible in search of a certain scripture.

Harbor rinsed the sink out then climbed into bed next to her. He thought about what Shiloh would say to the fact that he almost kissed Emily. The last thing he wanted was to stir feelings of insecurities within her. She was already battling overwhelming insecurities with her body and her pregnancy.

"Shi, I gotta tell you something."

She never looked up from her Bible. "I already know."

Shocked, Harbor tried to read the emotions on her face. She didn't seem mad. She didn't seem hurt. She didn't even look curious. "What do you know?"

She looked up from her Bible and into his face.

"When I invited Emily, she declined and told me her reason. At first, I was pissed. Like. Dude, you didn't even wait three months." She slapped his arm with the back of her hand. "But then I thought about how lonely I was, to the point of anticipating the sound of Jake's truck just so I'd have someone to talk to. I thought about how lonely you probably were." She held his hand. "If I can forgive Jake, how much more I should be able to forgive you, the man I'm crazy over?"

He stared at her speechless.

"What?" She asked.

He shook his head. "I don't deserve you."

"No, you don't," she teased. "But I don't deserve the grace Jesus extends to me. I vowed a long time ago to be merciful in my marriage just as Christ is merciful to me, and I've offended Him way worse than a little flirting offends me."

He took her face into his hands and kissed her passionately. Instead of her body turning rigid, she melted into him.

₨⃣

"Here babe." Shiloh stood at his bedside with his morning coffee. He cleared a spot for her to set the coffee cup on his nightstand. She set it down and climbed into the bed next to him. He pulled her into him.

"Thank you. For last night and for the coffee."

"Shut up," she teased.

He laughed at her embarrassment.

They laid cuddling, enjoying the silence before the kids woke up.

"I think I'm ready to tell the kids."

Harbor held her and waited.

"About the baby." She turned over to face him. "What do you think?"

He thought for a moment, "I think we'll be surprised at their response."

A look of confusion settled on her face.

"Momma, I wan' some coffee." Millie came in rubbing her eyes.

"Me, too." Junior was right behind her.

ৡৎৰ

"Ya'll pick up these toys. We're about to have guests over." Shiloh busied herself and the children with straightening up the house.

"She already knows how we live," Ann smarted as she picked up a baby doll.

"Ann," Shiloh said sternly.

"Yes, ma'am."

"Momma, someone's here." Nora looked out the blinds at Deputy's barking.

"Okay. Come on over here and finish picking up these game pieces."

Shiloh straightened up the crooked throw pillows on the couch before answering the knock on the door.

"Hey! Ya'll come on in." She opened the door.

Nino ran down the hall barking wildly at the sound of strangers' voices.

"Nino. No. Hush. Go lay down."

"Welcome to our chaos," Shiloh joked as she closed the door behind Emily and an attractive dark-haired young man. "Ya'll sit down." She showcased the couch.

"Girl, ya'll are fine. This is calm compared to what we're used to," Emily replied.

"Now, who is this?" Shiloh studied the young man.

"Oh, I'm sorry. This is my boyfriend, Joseph."

He flashed a wide smile. "Hey."

Harbor came in with Mille and Junior following with blackened hands.

"Oh, my. What happened?" Shiloh stared at the black hands.

"They helped me get the charcoal in the grill," Harbor laughed as he wiped his hands on a paper towel.

"Okay, y'all come on let's wash your hands." Shiloh began ushering them to the bathroom, "It's nice to meet you Joseph." She swung over her shoulder as he stood to shake Harbor's hand.

෮෮

"You gonna call the children in?" Shiloh handed Harbor the last cup finishing the loading of the dishwasher.

"Yeah. You ready?"

"Yeah…"

Harbor began to holler for the children, but she stopped him.

"Wait."

"What?"

"Let's pray first?"

"Okay." He took her hands and they bowed their heads.

"Gracious Father, please guide our words and reactions to the children's reactions. Help our family to embrace our new normal. In Jesus name, Amen."

"Amen," he exhaled.

Harbor called the children in and they all went into the living room, filling up the couch as Shiloh and Harbor stood in front of them.

She marveled at what God had used her to create. Each body formed within her, yet each so very different. She remembered with each pair of pink lines that emerged she wondered how she would be able to love another baby, but as her belly grew to make room for the growing baby,

171

her heart did as well. The love she felt for each of them dissipated the last of the anxiety she had over whether or not she would be able to love this baby.

"Momma and I have some exciting news."

"We're going to Disney World?" Ann exploded causing her siblings to erupt in excitement.

Shiloh looked at Harbor. "Well, this is going smooth."

"Hey. Y'all calm down," she said in her mom voice while clapping for their attention.

"We are not going to Disney," Harbor huffed.

Deflated, they quieted down.

"We're going to have a baby," Shiloh announced cautiously.

"A baby?" Ann looked to her daddy. "But I thought you were fixed like Nino?"

Shiloh couldn't contain her laughter at her daughter's comparison.

"Yes. But God is greater than anything man can do." Harbor avoided further explanation of the reproduction process.

Ann jumped up and ran over to kiss Shiloh's belly and Nora followed.

"I hope it's another baby sister," Nora exclaimed while a toothless grin broke across her face.

"No. No more girls. I want a boy baby. Like me and Daddy." Junior shook his head and pumped his hands. Shiloh could see the argument escalating when Ann began to chime in.

"Eh!" She waved her finger, "God will give us what we need. Not necessarily what we want but regardless, whatever the baby is, will be the perfect fit."

"Can we help pick out names?" Ann and Nora jumped up and down.

"Yes, yes. That's fine. Now y'all start getting ready for bed."

The older three took off arguing who would be getting in the bath first. Shiloh had lost Millie in the excitement. She looked to the couch where Millie had been sitting.

"Where's Millie?" she asked Harbor who shrugged his shoulders.

"She was just here. I was watching the older ones with you and didn't see her."

Shiloh started towards Millie's bedroom when she heard a small voice in the playroom.

Millie was struggling to pull something out from underneath a mountain of toys.

"Millie, baby. What are you doing?"

She swung over her shoulder and looked at her mother through her platinum bangs. She continued tugging on the thing until it dislodged and sent her falling to her bottom.

"Got it."

Shiloh chuckled. "What have you got?"

"I got dis." Millie drug it past Shiloh and into her room. Curious, Shiloh followed. Had Millie not heard her? Millie busied herself tugging on the bright pink and purple contraption.

"Millie did you hear what I said in there?"

"Yes'm." she continued pulling.

"What do you think about me having another baby?" Shiloh leaned against the doorframe. Millie was a brilliant tot but also equally as stubborn, with the majority of the time rejecting anything that wasn't her idea. Candy included.

Millie held up her hands in ta-da fashion.

"Oh. That's nice, Millie. But what do you think about another baby?"

She looked at Shiloh confused and looked back at her rectangle. Millie picked up her rectangle and turned it over which revealed the rectangle was a doll's playpen.

"Baby seeps with me," she announced.

Twenty-Three

The clamoring of plastic trays landing carelessly onto metal bars and hum of conversation from his fellow inmates intensified Jake's headache. He rubbed his hand over his buzz cut before picking his tray from the top of the leaning tower of cafeteria trays still warm to the touch from the sterilizing rinse they had gotten after breakfast and fell in the rapid growing lunch line.

Keeping his eyes focused on the puke green tray in his hands he shuffled along with the rest of the hungry inmates. All the voices and conversations melted together until he reached the beginning of the hot bar where questionable grey patties and dull brown gravy filled steamy silver pans.

"What? Not good enough for you?"

A muscle in Jake's jaw twitched and heat flashed his face at the familiar voice. It was the same voice he had heard shouting profanities into the darkness his first night in this place. Jake looked up, but the sight of Garcia adorning a hair net on his bald head and apron with serving sanitary gloves covering his tattooed knuckles, extinguished Jake's jets. He tried not to laugh.

"No, it's good." Jake wondered if Garcia knew how

ridiculous he looked. Surely not. Jake couldn't dream of instigating a fight or trying to intimidate anyone in such an outfit.

ജ兆

Jacob was lead through the maze of blocked walls and doors made of iron bars until he was ushered into a small, bright room with a table equipped with arm, leg, and chest straps which was positioned in the middle of the room facing the windows where a few family members of his victims looked on.

On the wall behind the table hung a clock whose ticking unnerved him. Each tick of the hand made his heart drop lower and his stomach draw up higher until it sat in his throat.

"Might as well get comfortable." The guard nodded towards the table.

As he laid down, the blinding lights overhead made his eyes squint. The clattering of the utensils on the compact metal table stand next to him confirmed what his squinting made him unsure of; the executioner preparing the lethal concoction. The unfamiliar man strapped him, and Jacob grunted at the pressure of the tightened straps across his chest.

"Too tight?"

Jacob nodded.

"Good." The man whispered as Jacob's vision became blurred with moisture and a warm, wet tear rolled down the crease of his eye just as the sharp pain of the needle broke through the crease in his arm.

"You won't feel anything. Just sleepy."

That was a lie.

The liquid lava rushing through his veins made him scream a blood curdling scream as it ran up his arm and into his shoulder. His body began convulsing causing him to writher on the table as a beheaded snake.

He could no longer hear his screams for the blood roaring in his ears. Flashes of heat burned his body from the inside out.

"HEEEELLLLP ME!" He shot up in the bed banging his forehead on the bunk above him.

He rubbed the goose egg that was beginning to bulge on his forehead with his trembling hands. He shuffled to the tin can of a sink and splashed his face with some water.

"Father, give me peace."

He looked to the calendar on his cell wall. One week until his nightmare could possibly become a reality. He shuddered at the thought.

He sat on the edge of his bed and picked up his worn Bible. He began reading as the thought crossed his mind that there was no peace for him this side of Heaven, but at least he could get lost in heavenly thinking.

₨₩

Turning down the radio at the ringtone of her phone she read the caller I.D. Her mouth dried up and she licked her lips to try to generate some spit.

"Hello?" She thought her tongue sounded like it clung to the roof of her mouth instead of rolling to produce the l's.

"Hey! Where'd ya go?"

She wanted to lie. She knew if she told him he would demand her to turn around. To forget the whole crazy idea. She drummed the steering wheel as she jumped back and

177

forth between a rock and a hard place.

"Babe? Can you hear me?"

"Yeah."

"Where'd ya go?"

"I'm… I'm headed to see Jake." The truth fell from her lips quicker than her mind could think up a lie. He wasn't supposed to call. He was supposed to have a schedule full of deliveries to make. Silence came from Harbor's end. "I know it's crazy, but I feel like I gotta check on him before… well, ya know."

"He suffers the consequences of his actions?"

"Yes, Harbor," she sighed.

"I don't know why! Shi, he was able to break out of his hospital room…I mean, I forgive him but I trust him alone with any woman as much as I would trust an alcoholic in a brewery."

She sighed, "I'll be fine."

"Shiloh. Be careful."

"I will. Love you."

"You know you could've told me. You didn't have to sneak off."

"Bye, Harbor. I love you," she said stern-like.

"Yeah, I love you, too."

She prayed she was wrong. Nightmares plagued her, taunting her that Jake's conversion was false. *Again.* She glanced at her GPS, only twenty-seven more miles and she'd be face to face with her attacker.

Once there, an Amazon of a female deputy ushered her into a room with a row of cubicles, each equipped with a glass panel, two-way phone, and chair.

"Station seven," the deputy commanded as she pointed to a cubicle on the far end with a number seven in black chipped paint.

Shiloh took her seat and waited for what felt like an eternity until she saw movement on the other side of the glass. First, a deputy and then Jake, followed by another deputy to whom he was conversing with. She tried regulating her breathing as it seemed as if all the air in the room escaped through the cracks of the mortar in the brick walls surrounding her.

Jake nodded as the deputy pointed to that station in which she sat. A look of surprise followed by remorse painted his face when he saw her sitting on the other side of the glass. He took the seat across from her.

She stared at him as he kept his eyes down and picked at the chipping paint on the table in front of him.

You didn't come to stare at him.

She tapped on the glass pane and pointed towards his phone as she picked up hers.

He nodded and brought the phone to his ear.

She swallowed hard. "Well… did you find Him?"

He smiled a faint smile. "Yeah… yeah, I did."

"Really?"

"Yeah… I, uh, I've actually been reading my Bible and sharing with some of the inmates. I figured I could still do something for The Lord as long as He's got me here." He shrugged.

Her eyes began to sting indicating tears, she rubbed them to avoid it.

"Jake, that's wonderful. Praise the Lord! I just hate that you're having to learn this way… in this place."

"Well, way I figured it is, just because I'm saved doesn't prevent consequences for my actions. Ya know, the day I went to the lake, I was going to take a welder that the company I worked for left out there and hock it. But there was you. God had different plans. I'm sorry that I had to learn that way."

She nodded.

"Besides, I may be imprisoned physically, but spiritually, I'm free. Thank you." He smiled.

She smiled back and hung the phone back on the receiver.

On the way home, the Spring showers had left a sweet smell trailing into her rolled down windows. She inhaled deep, savoring the mixture of rain and honeycomb.

Oh, God. Thank You. Thank You so much for redeeming Jake. Please be merciful tomorrow. Lord, let it be quick and painless. Empower him to be a witness for You up till You welcome him into Glory.

A sudden tinge of pain in her swollen abdomen made her gasp. She rubbed at it to try to ease its stinging. Her due date was creeping up fast and Braxton Hicks had made their appearance in each pregnancy prior. Only five more weeks and she would welcome the blessing produced out of her burden. She had only hoped for one thing, that the baby wouldn't favor his or her father.

Not long after she arrived home, Harbor nodded toward her round belly. "Did he ask about the baby?"

"No, I stayed in my seat until he left. I figured there was no reason for him to know."

"So… did you find out anything?" he asked as he pulled plates from the cabinet to set the table.

She nodded as she stuck her tongue to the wooden spoon covered with sauce.

"And?"

"He's ready. He's really saved, says he's been sharing with the other inmates too." She drained the noodles into a colander.

"Good."

Another bolt of pain shot across her belly almost causing her to drop the noodles into the sink. She inhaled sharply through clenched teeth.

"Hey. You okay?" Harbor came to her side.

"Yeah. Hand me a bottle of water and y'all go ahead and eat. I'm gonna lie down for a sec."

He handed her the water and watched her waddle from the kitchen.

"What's wrong with Momma?" Nora asked as the children took their seats at the dinner table.

"She ain't feeling good. She'll be alright though. This ain't her first rodeo." He scooped some noodles onto her plate.

"You've tossed and turned all night," Harbor sighed as he turned the lamp on that sat atop his nightstand.

She turned over to face him. "I'm sorry. I've got a killer headache and it's making me nauseous."

Harbor ran his hand through his hair. "Well. What do you need?"

She closed her eyes and shrugged. "What time is it?"

He glanced at the clock on his table. "3:19."

"If I'm not better in a couple of hours, I'm gonna call the doctor when they open."

"Okay. You want anything now?"

"No, just turn out that light and let's try to get some sleep."

Twenty-Five

Shiloh rolled out of bed at the crowing of the rooster. She tapped her phone to see the time only to have her focus redirected to her hot dog sized fingers.

She had never swelled to this extent during her previous pregnancies. *But I'm older now.* She looked at her ring finger. She immediately regretted it. The pain of her wedding band cutting off the circulation to her ring finger wasn't apparent until she thought about it. The idea of having to cut it off sent her breathing from a rhythmic hum into a frantic huffing. She waddled to the kitchen and squirted a glob of dish detergent onto her finger. She was twisting it back and forth frantically when Harbor stumbled in, sleep in his eyes.

"What are you doing?"

"I'm trying to get my ring off. My hands are swelling."

"Here lemme try." He pushed the puffiness of her finger down before yanking on the ring.

"OW!" she gasped. "Let go!"

"Don't be such a baby. I've almost got it."

She squirmed and he pulled. The ring finally popped off.

"UGH!" Shiloh huffed. "Thanks, but you nearly took

my finger off." She sulled up as she rubbed her sore finger.

"You're welcome." He dropped the ring in her open palm.

"How's your head?"

"Not much better."

"You gonna call?" He raised an eyebrow.

"Yes." She rolled her eyes but soon regretted it as dizziness set in. She held onto the sink, blinking long and slow.

"What's going on?"

"I-I dunno." The room spun and she lost her grip on the sink. Harbor grabbed her just before she fell to the floor.

"We ain't waiting. I'm taking you to the doctor. NOW."

ॐ

Jake's eyes stung as he read his Bible. He hadn't slept a wink the night before for fear of that reoccurring nightmare. He glanced at the clock on the wall. The jailer would be bringing him his last meal soon. His stomach was in knots, he doubted he would be able to eat it.

He focused on the words bound up in a maroon cover that sat in his lap. Jesus was about to die on the cross. Jake thought about God performing some kind of miracle preventing his execution. He had prayed for it. He prayed for it again.

"Father, I feel so distant from You. I don't feel comforted. Please send Your comfor-"

I wasn't comfortable.

Jake dropped off from praying and began to clear his mind, attempting to mediate on that thought.

"Jesus wasn't comfortable. He was very

uncomfortable, in fact. Yet He was still inside the perfect will of God. Jesus had even asked why God had forsaken Him. It's okay if I feel forsaken, because I know I am not. I am inside God's Will. I have repented and trusted in Him. I have ministered to others best I could. I'm not going to stop now. No matter how uncomfortable I am. My last few hours on Earth are not for me to grieve a life that isn't worth living, no, these last few hours are to glorify the eternal life with the eternal Father that I'm about to get to enjoy!"

Knock. Knock. Knock.

Detective Harris stepped in with his last meal.

The aroma of pancakes, bacon, grits, and eggs just like Pops used to make on Saturday mornings when he was just a boy made his stomach rumble. Then he wondered if he would see Pops in Heaven.

"Harris…what do you know about Jesus?"

හි

Harbor wheeled Shiloh into the emergency room as she sat unconscious in the wheelchair. "Help. Help me!" He rushed through the sliding doors at sign in.

"Sir. Come over here." An older woman as round as she was tall sat behind a computer and desk.

"Have you pre-registered?"

"What? I don't know. Is this not the emergency room?" He looked around the eerily quiet room.

"Yes, sir, but you have to be registered. Has she been here before?" She began clicking on the computer's mouse.

"What the Hell? Are you serious right now? My wife is pregnant and unconscious!"

"Harbor?" A familiar voice called his attention, saving

the receptionist a chewing out and Harbor's blood pressure. He turned to see Emily standing in the door that lead to the triage.

"Hey. Help me. She's unconscious."

"And pregnant!" She sprinted over and knelt beside Shiloh, lifting her limp wrist she checked her pulse and pulling her eyelids open, checked her pupils.

"Come on." She took the wheelchair and rushed to Shiloh to triage with Harbor on her heels.

೩)(೮

He followed Harris down the hall while answering different questions he had about what God had done in Jake's heart until they reached a pair of heavy doors at the end of the hall, where another deputy waited.

"This is where I leave you." Harris nodded.

Jake offered a wry smile as he took a deep breath. Before the doors shut behind him, Jake swung over his shoulder. "Seek Him. It's so freeing."

He saw Harris nod as the door closed.

Jake was led through the maze of blocked walls and doors made of iron bars, eerily similar to his nightmare, fear crept up his back, causing chills to break out across his skin. He inhaled with each step of his right foot and exhaled with each step of his left, while reciting Psalms 23 until he was ushered into a small, bright room with a table equipped with arm, leg, and chest straps. It was positioned in the middle of the room facing the windows where a few family members of his victims looked on.

On the wall behind the table hung a clock whose ticking unnerved him. Each tick of the hand made his heart drop lower and his stomach draw up higher until it sat in his throat.

He laid on the table as his head hit the pillow, a blanket of comfort covered him, and a spirit of thankfulness filled him. He began singing aloud a hymn he had forgotten but his heart had remembered from when he was a young boy sitting on the church pew between Maw and Pops.

Sweet hour of prayer
Sweet hour of prayer
May I thy consolation share.
Till, from Mount Pisgah's lofty height

He saw the jail's general practitioner wielding a needle come close and he shut his eyes tight.

I view my home and take my flight,
This robe of flesh, I'll drop and rise.
To seize the everlasting prize,
And shout while passing through the air.

He felt a prick in his arm and the warmth of a tear running down his temple into his hair.

Farewell, Farewell,
Sweet hour of prayer.

A warmth flowed up his arm.

ഇറ

"Mr. Romans?' Dr. Stephens waved Harbor to come to him as he whispered something to a nurse who nodded and dismissed herself to enter back into Shiloh's room.

Emily patted his back as he rose and before he could blink, he was already standing eye to eye with the doctor.

"Yeah?" He crossed his arms over his chest and squared up his feet as if he was steadying himself for a blow.

"Harbor, it's not looking good. Her blood pressure was 80/100."

"Ok. You're gonna have to put it in layman's terms for me."

"Stroke-level."

Harbor stood but wondered if he was on the floor because it was as if he had been kicked in the chest by a mule. All the sterilized air had been sucked out of the hall in which he stood. Before he could catch his breath to ask another question, the nurse pushed Shiloh's door opened and hollered for the doctor.

ℰᴑᴁ

Shiloh heard someone by her bedside. She peeked through squinted eyelids. Her head pulsated. A nurse was adjusting some numbers on her I.V. monitor.

She closed her eyelids tight to slow the spinning room and her eyes' rapid movements.

She began to breathe faster as the fear of losing consciousness overwhelmed her. She tried to fight her body from convulsions and her jaw tightening. Before she lost consciousness, she heard her door opening and hitting the wall behind it with a thud and what seemed like a panicked whisper, "She's seizing."

ℰᴑᴁ

All fear and pain evaporated in the wake of a brilliant light and a comforting warmth filled the atmosphere. A terrifying yet breathtakingly beautiful voice called out, *"Well done, My good and faithful servant."*

Twenty-Six

The baby bundled up in the soft blanket let out a cry that sounded more like a kitten mewing.

"Aw, it's ok Atlan. Momma's got you." She breathed in the addictive scent of newborn as she nuzzled the baby's neck. The baby quieted down at the voice of his mother. Shiloh smiled at the contentment that overwhelmed her.

"Atlan. That's a beautiful name. Where'd you come up with that?" the nurse asked as she checked Shiloh's vitals.

"It means new beginnings." Shiloh smiled.

"Alright, alright. Let me hold my boy." Harbor tucked the baby into his arms like he was the winning football.

He stared into his small, porcelain face as he caressed his plump cheek with his calloused thumb and sighed, "He looks just like his momma."

The End

About the Author

Stephanie lives in Alabama with her husband and four children, four dogs, and chickens. She enjoys studying her Bible, sharing her findings with whoever will listen, encouraging women to a deeper relationship with Christ, dancing, and being outdoors. Stephanie is also a speaker, *"Rough Girl Turned Redeemed"*, she shares real, raw, and relevant truths of faith, marriage, and motherhood in person or on her blog:

https://roughgirlturnedredeemed.com/

and her podcast:

Rough Girl Turned Redeemed by Stephanie Holbrook.

You can reach out to her at

Stephanie@roughgirlturnedredeemed.com.

Acknowledgements

Well, I know I'm going to forget someone but we've gotta wrap this bad boy up. First and foremost, thank you to my hubby who wouldn't let me quit. I had so much fun working out the details of this story with you over late-night snacks.

To "my friends in my phone," Annette, Emilee, Kitty, and Aimee. Words cannot describe what ya'll are to me. Can't wait 'til we're neighbors in Heaven!

To Mr. Jon, Scooter, Thad, Ashley, and Margaret for allowing me to pick your brains on all things dealing with detective work, medical procedures, and legal proceedings. This book couldn't have happened without your help!

To my therapist, Dr. Trader, who counseled me through so much and encouraged me to keep going and to keep writing.

To my girl, Whitney, for encouraging, challenging me, and being beside me for all the adventures writing has taken me. Here's to many more late-night cookie runs and viral articles!

To my Aunt Rose who prayed for me.

To my Momma who toted me to the library all those summer days as a child, igniting the love for reading which lead to writing.

To my editor and publisher, Ellen Sallas, for

making this dream come true and making it look *waaaaay* better than I imagined!

Lastly and most importantly, my ABBA, Who laid this story on my heart and didn't let my fears and insecurities hinder His work through me. If you loved the story, that's all Him, if you didn't, that's on me. He receives all the glory forever and ever. Amen.